SWEET SIN SLAUGHTERHOUSE

A SAPPHIC EROTIC HORROR

THE DEVIL'S SOCIETY

KINSLEY KINCAID

ISBN eBook: 978-1-998646-08-1

ISBN Paperback: 978-1-998646-09-8

Editing: Rumi Khan

Proofreading: Daisie Mae - Editing & Proofreading

Cover Design: Artista Grafico

"Fuck the Patriarchy."

- Dr. Taylor Alison Swift

"My teeth, my car, my vagina, my business."
- Kelly Osbourne

NOTE FROM THE AUTHOR

Please be aware this book contains many dark themes and subjects that may be uncomfortable/unsuitable for some readers. This book contains **heavy themes** throughout. Please keep this in mind when entering *Sweet SIN Slaughterhouse*. Content warnings are listed on authors' social pages & website.

This book and its contents are entirely a work of fiction. Any resemblance or similarities to names, characters, organizations, places, events, incidents, or real people are entirely coincidental or used fictitiously.

If you find any genuine errors, please reach out to the author directly to correct it.
Thank you.

This book is intended for 18+ only.

READING ORDER

The Devil's Society

Elijah's Duet;
Haunted by the Devil
Homecoming
*Sinner; Before Rain - Prequel**

Nathaniel's Story;
Unholy

Sid Sinclair;
Sweet SIN Slaughterhouse

*Can be read before, between or after the duet.

PLAYLIST

Party in the U.S.A - Miley Cyrus
Boss Bitch - Doja Cat
Little Girl Gone - CHINCHILLA
Dancing On My Own - Calum Scott
Someone You Loved - Lewis Capaldi
High Infidelity - Taylor Swift
Wrecking Ball - Miley Cyrus
Fuck The Pain Away - Peaches
Guess featuring Billie Eilish - Charli xcx
Ice Cream (with Selena Gomez) - BLACKPINK
Who's Afraid Of Little Old Me? - Taylor Swift
Don't Mess With Me - Brody Dalle
Bad Romance - Lady Gaga
Breakin' Dishes - Rihanna
Kill This Love - BLACKPINK
Mean (OG or TV) - Taylor Swift
10 Things I Hate About You - Leah Kate

Kick It - Peaches
Girls (fest. Cardi B, Bebe Rexha, Charli xcx) - Rita Ora
Judas - Lady Gaga
FEMININE ENERGY - COBRAH
Prayer Of The Refugee - Rise Against
Descending - Sleep Token
SPOTIFY PLAYLIST

HIERARCHY

Diablo(s)
NATHANIEL/ SID

Antichrist(s)
DARRIAN

Demons
ELIJAH   ROGERS

THOMAS   RAIN   RYLEE

Hellhounds
WINSTON   LUCY

TASH

The Damned

NEW INITIATES BLOOD OR CIVILIAN

1

SID

"I can't hear you!" Shouting many octaves above the soundtrack playing in my ears.

Rolling my eyes, I turn around and scan the table. My fingers tingle with excitement at all the options before me, but my eyes keep drifting back to one in particular, a long, thin piece of beautiful bronze, with a slight hook at the end. Very similar to a crochet hook, but much cooler and *far* more deadly.

Biting my lip as my fingertips graze the cool metal, tingles electrify throughout my body in excitement. My pussy clenches and my eyes hood knowing what is to come, and it gets me so fucking horny.

Slowly, I slide my white crystal-encrusted gas mask down my face, my long and bejeweled black nails rake across each bump and ridge. With each click, it adds to the suspense and tension radiating in my tunnel.

The sweet melody of "Party in the USA" by Miley Cyrus is playing on repeat, but I pause it so I can hear the precious symphony of the screams one last time. Removing the headphone off my ear slightly, I turn around, bronze hook in hand, and take in my latest slaughterhouse casualty.

She's naked.

Legs bent at the knee, similar to a squat position, ass up and arms strapped behind her, wrists chained to the ceiling. Her head hangs forward, her ankles shaking, and the tension is taut against the chain. At any moment, the traitor's shoulders could pop out of the sockets—an excruciating pain, I imagine. And fucking hope.

Pulling the rope hanging next to me once more, a bucket of ice-cold water rains down on her. I've been told it feels like a thousand sharp knives digging into your skin, and in her case, spine. The back is very sensitive, full of nerves. The perfect spot for this technique.

I don't want her to talk, because I know everything I need to. I want her to suffer. I want her to hurt and regret ever betraying my family and The Devil's Society.

"Suzzie Q, was it worth it?" I taunt, my words muffled by the mask. Cries echo throughout the cement cylinder as her body shivers and her toes spasm against the dirt and rocks.

Her name isn't Suzzie, but she isn't worth her name anymore.

She is a pest. An annoying little cockroach who I keep

stepping on, drowning with ice bucket after ice bucket, but she just won't die.

She and her family hate us. They, for some fucking reason, have an allegiance to the dead and defeated. The cowards and deranged. There is a small group in town who keep trying to revive the legacy of The Exiled, even if they know what we are capable of. But it never fails; everyone wants to be a hero. They sent this one in as a new recruit; they thought she'd get in undetected, but she couldn't have been more obvious. Always asking questions and always the first to volunteer. We passed on some bullshit information to her and waited. The Exiled took the bait, and we confirmed the mole.

My dad and I watched in the woods as the small group thought they were about to attack some vulnerable society members, but the area was empty, and they knew then they had been found out. But as the cowards they are, they left her to die. No attempt at a rescue mission. She was just another pawn in their game.

My dad and Papa have told me that those who are still loyal to The Exiled are those who were related to Brad and Dalton, or those still living off the cash left behind. They are a small group, an annoying group, actually, who take up our resources in humoring their playtime, when we have real shit to run.

A couple fluorescents hang throughout the tunnel, but the light is dim, shadows casting over her pathetic face. Her head hangs as her entire body is now engulfed in one massive shiver. The teeth chattering has begun to annoy me, so I slip my headphones back on. Miley Cyrus greets me once more. What a banger. And the perfect song for my next performance. Because I'm about to fucking party in here.

Stepping toward her in my black combat boots, I tilt my head and take in the pathetic pest. Bending at the waist, I feel a cool drift of air on my backside from being suddenly exposed. I'm in a short black plaid schoolgirl skirt, my legs bare, and a black torn cropped tee, with no panties on. They are far too restricting.

My sharp, pointed fingernail drags down the side of her damp cheek, hard. Warm blood counters the coolness of her skin, and I think this is what it must feel like in South Africa, where the Atlantic meets the Indian Ocean, hot versus cold, the ultimate battle for dominance. And I love it.

Twisting the once cool but now warm bronze between my thumb and forefinger in my other hand adds another element to my analogy. I ponder for a moment before smirking.

Heat always wins.

I am a Demon's daughter and Diablo's grandchild; heat runs through my veins.

Nothing could be more perfect.

Holding her chin firm, I tilt her face up toward me and take her in one last time. What a shame; she is so pretty like this, nipples hard as her stomach muscles contract, and tears join the stream of blood running down her face. I shaved her head earlier in the day because I didn't like it long. She is far more beautiful without it, raw and bare.

Looking up at me, my pest pleads once more with her eyes, so sad and pathetic.

Winking, I give a half smile she won't be able to see under my mask as I move swiftly, shoving the hooked bronze rod up her nostril and past her sinus. Things get a bit tricky the higher I get, so I angle her head back toward the ground and knee the rod, thus pushing it farther up her nose and into her brain. Only an inch of bronze is left to be seen. Tilting her head back up, blood has begun trickling out of her mouth, nose, and now her eyes. Gripping the tool, I slowly rotate it so the hook can begin attaching itself to her brain tissue. The more I turn, the more resistant it becomes. Carefully, I wiggle the bronze hook down, not wanting to lose anything on the other end. This is my take on the ancient Egyptian process of mummification, just one of the many steps to their process. I don't have time to fulfill and honor all aspects of the ritual, so I pay my respects by adapting bits and pieces of their technique.

As I pull the hook out, a large piece of brain matter comes with it. Giddy with excitement, I take a moment and examine it. White tissue with red blood encasing it, the sharp hook severed this piece beautifully.

Looking down at my pest, her tongue is hanging out and drool drips from her chin to the gravel floor. I push the tool up once more, and this time it's easier; just a bit of elbow grease and I am back inside her head. Twirling my tool around, I hum along to sweet Miley as I pull another piece out of her nose. More blood pours out of her and begins to pool at my feet.

Before I can continue, my phone rings through the headphones, interrupting my song. Assholes.

"What?" I snark, annoyed.

"It's time. She won't make it past this evening," my dad says, and instantly my heart sinks into the pit of my stomach. If it were up to him, he would have just taken her out long ago. Mom would have never allowed it, and surely she is the only reason he's calling me now. Daddy is different; he truly tries when it comes to me and feelings, I've seen it, but he just doesn't know any better.

Clearing my throat, I attempt to mask my emotions and respond, "Yeah. Okay. I'll be there soon." Then hang up. I'm not wanting to prolong the uncomfortable conversation. I know how hard even calling me about it was for the both of us.

Dropping the hook to the ground, it lands in a sea of crimson. Closing my eyes and lifting my mask off my face, I take a deep breath in, pinching my mouth shut. I keep it held in for as long as I can before exhaling. With my mask in hand, which now feels like the weight of the world, I walk to the table and place it down before sulking and looking over my shoulder. "Suppose you're dead now too."

Letting my raven black hair down from my high pony,

it falls to just above my backside. And as I shake my hair out, a single tear escapes from my eye.

It's the only piece of visual emotion I'll ever allow.

Mumbling to my pest, I say, "I'll have to hang you from the cathedral's peak later."

My heart aches in denial, and dare I say it's finally time to go say the final goodbye.

2

SID

"Where's your girlfriend, Brenda?"

"You know that's not her fucking name, Blaise."

"I do. But I don't care."

I won't let my baby brother get to me today. No one will stomp on me publicly, even though internally I'm already crippled.

Standing outside, the breeze is warm as the summer sun begins to set. Wearing a vintage black velvet pillbox cap with a black lace veil that stops just above my chin; traditionally called a widow's cap, I turn my attention away from Blaise and toward the gravesite before us in my parents' backyard.

"Why are you even dressed like that?" He can't stand not being the center of attention. Rolling my eyes, I don't turn around or respond to his ignorant question. Along with my widow's cap, I am dressed in a black Victorian mourning dress. A high neckline is latched together with a gold brooch that Greta gifted me on my eighteenth birthday. My lip quivers from the memory. My arms are covered, and the bodice is tight, a corset embroidered with intricate detailed lace overtop the flat black fabric. Looking down at my bare feet, the only part of bare skin visible on me, they peek out from under the long gown that flows from the corset, my toes curling against the earth, grounding me.

My lace-covered hands hold on to the two leashes just a little tighter, knowing how easy it is to lose a loved one.

My precious pink with black-spotted babies, Jack and Sally Jr., oink while digging their noses into the soil next to me. Flappy ears cover their eyes, and I often wonder how they are able to see, but they do. I spend hours watching them in the yard, my pride and joy.

Their parents, Millie and who I thought was Sally but turned out to be Sal, produced many heirs, but these two were the last of the bunch before Sal died just days before Greta gave me my brooch. Engraved into it is Sal's face, so I can always keep him close. I raised them both since birth, and they will always be a part of me.

It's been nearly two years, and I still get emotional over it.

Clearing my throat, I acknowledge Blaise. "Abi is at work. On a job. She hasn't checked her phone... She doesn't know." Pausing, I know now is not the time to start an argument, but I poke the bear anyway. I suppose it's to take my mind off the overwhelming grief that's about to smack us all in the face, or knowing my family, only my mom and me.

"Why are you so miserable all the time?"

"Would the two of you shut up?" Dad yells from across the yard, shovel in hand, accompanied by his 'and I will use it on you' face.

I know he would never, as he's been giving us this look since we were kids. Mom would kick his ass if anything happened to either of us. She's always been our life insurance policy, and Greta's.

Catching myself smirking, I shift my face back to a somber expression.

"Elijah Sinclair!" Mom shouts, walking behind Dad. He waves her off as if there is nothing to worry about, but I know in a mere three seconds there will be.

"Why didn't you ever make Mom an official Sinclair?"

And here we go.

Closing my eyes, I brace myself, as I hear the scuffle take off behind me.

Dad likely has charged at my brother for insulting his queen. A pastime Blaise has gotten very good at. He doesn't discriminate, though, no, he is very good at insulting all of us.

A loud thud shakes the ground beneath me. My eyes prod open. Shifting my sight, I see Blaise is in a losing battle. Dad is on top of him, tattooed hand around my brother's throat, and I can almost guarantee that his eyes have turned from blue with brown specks to the darkest shade of black.

Dad grits out, "You will never speak of your mother or any other member of this family like that again. Your mother is fucking mine." I can feel the venom dripping from each word as he speaks. "She is more of a Sinclair than you will ever be."

"Elijah! Stop, you're going to kill him." Mom is the only one who can break the trance once my dad gets too deep into the dark depths of his soul.

My pigs snort, pacing, agitated by the outburst.

Taking my mom in, she stands tall, strong and confident, but I see past that and note the pain that is clearly displayed in her eyes. Something the guys would never notice or think their bickering would cause. Pain.

Dad is still focused on Blaise, but I see her. She feels it as our eyes connect warmly, for only a second.

Blinking rapidly, her mask appears just as she reaches the boys, who are none the wiser to the pain they have both caused her. She's the best woman I know, but she will never tell them, always protecting them over herself.

Forever selfless.

Dad gets up first, dusting himself off, followed by Blaise, who acts unfazed, but perhaps he feels the deepest. This will destroy him later, and in return, he will destroy himself. He will push everyone who loves him further away and convince himself he isn't worthy by forcing others to say it to him.

Mom's warm embrace encompasses me; the fresh scent of her floral perfume is comforting.

"Let's get this old bitch in the ground."

Dad isn't trying to be funny; this is genuinely how he deals with everything. Emotional intelligence is nonexistent in this man.

"E, please. Try to show some compassion. This is hard for some of us."

I lean into mom, thankful for her presence.

"I don't get why I'm here. It's just a fucking pig," Blaise mumbles, and Dad is quick to take the opportunity to lay another one on him.

"Don't speak of your grandmother that way in front of your mom and sister."

Looking over, both men have their arms crossed over their chests; it's something they do when they are pleased with themselves but don't want to show it.

"I'll bury you both in that fucking hole if I hear another word, you fucking Neanderthals."

Smiling, that voice is music to my ears. It's nails to a chalkboard to others, but never to mine.

Greta.

"Show some respect for the dead. Millie was a member of this family. Her children are here, grieving, while you two roll about on the ground. Fucking embarrassing." She continues.

Once reaching us, the lowering sun catches her walker in just the right light. Yellow crystals shine beautifully, it's captivating, as the glimmer dances around us.

"Millie knows you will take good care of her babies. She and Sal are reunited. No tears, my girl. Only happy memories." I've been sworn to secrecy. Only Rylee, Mom, and I get to see this soft, comforting side of Greta. She has a reputation to uphold, after all.

"Do you want to say any words?" Mom asks, but I shake my head no. I've said what I have needed to as she passed lying next to me in her pen earlier this evening.

Taking that as their signal to proceed, Dad and Blaise begin to push the heavy black tarp where Millie rests into the grave that is next to Sal's; the only two marked graves we have in our family compound.

Bending down, I grab the shovel Dad dropped while battling my brother, then pass the leash to my babies for Greta to hold on to. Looking down in the hole one last time, I nod and silently thank her for being mine and for giving me such joy while learning about life with my dad all these years.

Sticking the shovel into the pile of soil, I take one scoop and sprinkle it on top of her before stepping back and passing it back off to my dad.

I appreciate my family. They don't have to be here; they don't need to humor me like this, but they do. Even my brother, who acts like he hates all of us and everything.

And even my dad's one friend, Thomas, messaged me sending his condolences. It's strange that Papa and Rylee aren't here, but perhaps business called, which I completely understand, as they are the heads of The Devil's Society.

Papa is already counting the days down until his retirement; he says he has missed many precious important moments and doesn't want to miss any more. The time is approaching faster than I expected, and a tiny part of me wishes time would slow down for many reasons, but lately there's been just one on my mind. It's an overwhelming situation, being prepped to become the next Diablo of The Devil's Society.

My grandfather has built such a legacy, an empire with Rylee, D, and my dad by his side. All are shoes I fear can never be filled. Shoes I am not worthy of even attempting to fill.

I am terrified.

But now is not the time to stress or be anxious over things that haven't happened yet. I will save that for tomorrow. Because tomorrow is one day closer to the rest of my life.

Before I get too far gone into my thoughts, I casually inform the family, "The pest is dead in my tunnel. She's all yours if you want her." I had hopes of hanging her high from the peaks of the church, to make an example of, but I need to distract my brother from destroying himself later, even if he doesn't deserve my generosity. Papa has always said that a good leader can see their opponents' moves before they do. Blaise isn't my opponent, but he is a challenge, and my brother.

If he won't save himself, I can't either, but I can try and prolong his life just a tiny bit longer.

Reaching out, Greta places the black leather leashes back into my gloved hands. "Now, go kick some ass, girl."

So with my head raised and my middle finger held high, my girls and I begin our short walk home.

Not sure I'll be kicking any ass tonight, but I'll definitely be licking some pussy.

3

SID

"Oh fuck." Abi's eyes roll into the back of her head as sweat drips down her thick thighs. Lowering my head back down, I inhale deeply, and the smell of her sweet skin tickles my nose. My lips are as swollen as hers as I kiss them before lapping her clit with my tongue. Three fingers continue to work her pulsating pussy; I took off a couple of my nails so I wouldn't tear her cunt apart with them.

Heavy breathing continues. "Fuck, baby... There. Don't stop," Abi moans as if I haven't done this to her a hundred times before. I know what makes my girl tick. Her legs, which are hanging over my shoulders, move to wrap around my neck tightly.

She's almost there, and I smirk to myself in satisfaction.

As her pelvis begins to grind, using my face to get off, I wrap my lips around the devil's doorknob and suck hard. Abi's cunt grips my fingers tightly, my teeth teasing her sensitive nerves and sending her to the brink.

Just as her body tenses, I move my mouth and prepare for her sweet nectar. Tremors follow, Abi's legs vibrate around me, and her fingers grip my hair, yearning for control that I will not relent.

Cum coats my fingers, and before her orgasm subsides, I pull them out of her and replace them with my mouth and tongue. I lap her relentlessly, with the need to milk every last drop out of her. I'm fucking feral as my taste buds ignite in satisfaction. The harder she pulls my hair, the more I crave making her weak for me. Giving in to me and every fucking desire.

She doesn't own me. I own her.

Her body begins to relax as I hollow my cheeks and begin sucking her cum out.

But I don't swallow.

Moving my face back slightly, I look up, through my long lashes I find her green eyes. White blonde hair is fanned out all around her glowing body, and her nipples are hard. Tickling up Abi's beautiful legs, I grip her thighs and gently move them off my shoulders before placing her legs down on either side of me.

Leaning forward, I see her nipples are hard as my breasts skim along her skin, goosebumps following, as she shivers. My pouty lips connect to hers, and I feed her. A low groan follows from her throat as she devours her own release. My pussy aches in satisfaction.

Whispering against her lips, my words are soft but

true, "See, this is why I am so fucking addicted to you. You taste like Sunday mornings outside, after the midnight rain."

"I love you, Sin," she whispers back.

Sin is short for Sinclair. When I was little, people would call me baby Sin, because I am so much like my daddy, but behind it all, I have a lot of my mom in me too.

I kiss my girl hard before sitting up and admiring the curvy perfection sprawled out before me.

I've never been one to say it back, as verbalizing affection has always made me feel uncomfortable. You will know how I feel by my actions. And these actions, which have resulted in cum dripping down my chin, help show her how much I care.

My focus stays on her as racing thoughts begin to consume me.

We've been together for a couple of years and every part of me wishes that this, and us, will stay like this for a few decades more. That nothing will taint us, the spark won't dull and that love will conquer all. I refuse to let my job kill us.

These thoughts of optimism, happiness and the future help mask the memories of pain from this afternoon. Suppression at its finest. But I do wish my dreams for us come true.

"Baby, let's go on a date tomorrow, just you and me," I blurt out. Abi giggles, nodding her head yes. Leaning over her, my lips brush against hers. "What? Too tired to speak?" I tease back, and just before she can respond, a phone vibrates on the nightstand.

Closing my eyes, I'm annoyed. Today has been one of the hardest days, and all I wanted to do was to get lost in my girlfriend's pussy and then take her on a fucking date.

"It's mine," she mumbles, knowing I'm pissed.

I know it's fucking hers. It's always her phone going off.

When I take over things, I will be amending her work schedule drastically, because this is bullshit.

The hard plastic grinds against the wood surface like nails running slowly against a chalkboard as it continues to vibrate- knowing I fucking hate that sound. It makes my blood boil, only adding to my frustration. Clenching my fists, I use every ounce of energy I have to not punch another hole into the wall behind her.

Abi sighs, picking the phone up and reading the message. "I have to go."

Obviously.

"It's work. If anyone should understand, it's you." Ouch. Her words sting and a direct reaction to my attitude.

The low blow is fair, but it doesn't mean I have to like it.

"I know. I just..." I pause to gather my thoughts... my feelings. "I just needed you today." I squeeze my eyes tighter as images of Millie rotate in my mind.

You will not cry. You are not a pussy, I keep repeating to myself.

The bed shifts, a soft hand cup my face and whispers of reassurance follow. "I know, baby. I promise I will make it up to you. I always do, don't I?" Her voice goes all cutesy, something I can never resist. I nod as she kisses my forehead gently and whispers against my skin, "I love you."

We stay like this for a few moments. I feel so good, my body is warm from her connection. Abi calms me like no one else can.

Then like that, she is gone. The warmth follows her and I am now all alone.

Her feet pad against the hardwood floor, followed by the closing of the bathroom door. Falling forward onto the mattress, I cuddle into myself, naked, needing to get lost in the comfort of her scent left behind on the pillow. Heavy eyes stay closed as I begin to drift away. Exhaustion wants to take over, and today, I allow it, just this once.

The slamming of the front door awakens me from my unconscious state. My body is heavy, fully relaxed on top of the bedsheets where I lay, still naked. Opening my eyes, I peek around the room. It's dark and quiet. The only sound audible is that of my pigs sleeping peacefully in their beds only feet away from me. Before I allow my body to return to sleep, my bladder has another plan. Annoyed, I crawl out of bed and begin to make my way over to the bathroom. Before I'm able to make it all the way, my phone goes off this time.

"Fuck's sake."

Turning around, I search the bed until I find it. The

bright light is almost blinding. Squinting as my eyes adjust, I see it's Papa.

BOSS MAN

All heads meeting.

SALUTING THE PHONE, then scratching my head, I mutter, "Aye, aye, captain." Before replying back to him;

BOSS BITCH

Roger that, Papa bear.

HE DOESN'T RESPOND, surely too busy rounding up the rest of the crew.

Throwing my phone down, I spin and head to the bathroom and flick the light on. Looking in the mirror, I am disheveled, a fucking mess, actually. Mascara smudged all down my cheeks, lipstick stained around my mouth with dry cum, and my eyebrows are fucking gone.

Papa is going to have to wait because this bitch needs a shower.

Looking over myself once more, I shake my head, I wonder if they realize what they have gotten themselves into with me.

They have been training me my entire life, and *this*

is who I am. And I am going to take advantage of this tiny allowance of wiggle room while I can, to be just on time.

As the next leader of The Devil's Society, giving in to sleep, grief, or anything other than my work will never be an option again.

SKIPPING out of the house in my platform high-tops and a tight white tee tucked into my nineteen fifties high-waisted black shorts embellished with gold buttons, rustic Victorian lanterns greet me, lining my driveway with candles. The night's warm breeze dances along my skin and through my hair, which is in small victory rolls and long waves. I inhale the evening's fresh scent of mountain air and stand in the moment until I exhale.

Solace.

Opening my eyes, I look around the property, my little piece of land within the big scheme of things. On my family's estate, I take in the beauty I've surrounded myself with. Large hanging willow trees, black iron fencing to match the outdoor furniture, old yard sculptures which most would call morbid, and cobblestones. All of which bring me immense joy.

Walking down the wide stone steps, a white piece of paper on the hood of my black Bentley SUV catches my attention, causing me to pause.

My finger taps my chin. Color me curious.

Strolling closer, my eyes squint through my oversized black cat-eye glasses, which are purely for aesthetics.

Interesting.

Reaching across the hood to the naked body on top of it, I yank the paper from the grips of the staples. Shaking off the excess blood, I see the edges have been burnt and the writing is done in ash.

We see you when you're sleeping.

ROLLING MY EYES, I fold the delicate paper and slide it into my front pocket. Moving around to the other side of my car, I take hold of the long bright pink hair which has become familiar to me. A new initiate. She joined the society by choice and was on her way to go places with us. She *was* a favorite among the pharma groups.

She is, or was, Tash; rest in peace. I do the catholic cross over my chest out of respect, I don't do religion, but maybe she did?

This girl sold better than pharma's own sales reps could here. And because of that, she helped us in landing the highest percentage of the take anyone has ever had in our town's history. The one pharma group we allow in, can sell to our hospital, pharmacies, and physicians, but we demand a fat stack of cash, demanding forty-five percent of the profit.

And we only had one rule: No Opioids.

And if they didn't like our terms, we would make their demise painful while smiling as we watched them burn. They all know, if we take a meeting, it's a gift, an opportunity that we could give to millions of other pharmaceutical companies. They would jump for the chance of gaining our territory, but if we take your meeting, you listen and you accept it. Papa was prepared to ask for twenty-five percent, Tash interjected, said fuck that, and closed at fourty-five.

What a fucking shame. It will take another lifetime to find someone like her again.

She was rare.

There are many different unspoken rules you learn growing up in the society, and one of the biggest is, you can't grow attached to people in this lifestyle. People come and go, funerals and unmarked graves are the norm, but shit, she fucking had a young child with no dad in the picture.

Peering closer at her exposed body, just below her breasts is a large incision. Two lines make one upside-down cross. The small Devil's Society brand, which was so beautifully decorating her abdomen is gone, replaced by a circle of shredded skin and exposed muscle. Looking down, I gaze at mine on the palm of my hand, allowing my mind to wander- as it often does, naturally.

The OGs of the society aren't marked, it's something initiates, also known as 'The Damned' started doing a few years ago. I wanted to show how serious I was about making this my life, so I joined them one night and got it in the worst imaginable place. Hurt like a motherfucker, but I earned their respect with one simple gesture. It's one thing I will never regret, never.

As the memory fades, so does the phantom pain that begins to throb at the thought of it all. Moving closer, my eyes squint and my nose scrunches, "What a fucking mess," I mumble in disgust to myself. The fresh cuts along Tash's flesh have been cauterized, making it impossible to tell what kind of knife or tool made the incision. Meaning, I may never know who did this.

Examining the rest of her, I can't make out any other wounds thanks to the dim lighting. Just the staples left behind from the note remain, a glint of shine bounces off the moonlight.

Removing my glasses, I bite the plastic arm and stare off into the dark distance of the night. Raising my brows, I tap my toe, curious indeed.

4

SID

Papa's house is only down the street. Walking through his front door, loud voices echo down the hall. Rylee's head pokes out. "Sid, we're all in here." I've always liked her. My dad doesn't share the same sentiment. I think it's because they could technically be siblings with the age difference. She and Papa have been together for nearly twenty years, if not more, and never married. Which I totally support, because at the end of the day, it's just a fucking piece of paper. Mom and dad are the same.

They are all endgame and I am obsessed.

I love reading people, watching people, because the human mind is fascinating. Papa may wear the pants in the family business but she makes him beg for it in the bedroom. Knowing them better than others, I can just tell. And it makes me even more proud to be a member of this sadistic family.

Walking into the office, I'm greeted by Greta on the recliner off in the corner. Delacroix, Cecilia, Rylee, Rogers, Thomas, and my parents are a few familiar faces lining the room on top of the handful of non-family members.

Sitting behind his desk, cigar in hand with two fingers of whiskey in a crystal glass before him, is my grandfather, Nathaniel Sinclair. A leather chair sits next to him, so leisurely I walk past everyone and take my seat next to him. I wonder how one would acquire a throne, I'm not pretentious or think I am better than anyone, but the aesthetic appeals to me. As I lower myself to the chair, the paper in my pocket crinkles. Fuck.

Pulling it out, I discreetly and inconspicuously place it on Papa's lap, out of sight and out of mind. My focus stays ahead to not draw attention. This is a matter not up for a group discussion, so no need to alarm anyone if it's nothing at all. Papa snatches it like a pro while his deep voice echoes in the room,

"It's no secret that by the close of this year, Sid Sinclair will be the new Diablo of The Devil's Society. Starting tonight, right fucking now, all communication goes to both of us. If I catch one message differing between the two of us, consider your days numbered. I won't tolerate bullshit politics or gender profiling. If anything, you should be goddamn terrified to piss her off considering who her daddy is. Do I make myself crystal fucking clear?"

It's rare to see Papa this formally commanding. But

that's how you know he isn't messing around. This is one hundred percent serious and any violation of his order will land you in an unmarked grave. The corners of my mouth attempt to smirk, the thought of killing gives me great thrill, but I then remind myself, these are our own, and it would be devastating.

No one objects, the room sits silent, and all eyes remain focused on us. He has the ability to command everyone's attention and keep it.

"Good. Now that we have that covered, high-level updates." Papa snaps his fingers and sits back in his chair, sucking back on his cigar with his eyes on Greta, giving her a curt nod to begin.

"Similar to Nathaniel, I have decided it's time to step back completely from The Ranch. I'm getting too old to deal with small dicks. Rylee has fully stepped in since the rebuild and I will officially transfer the deed to the house, licenses, and land into her name within the week." Greta smiles with pride and the room claps, congratulating Rylee while also celebrating Greta. She's a fucking icon. I wish she would write an autobiography one day, because I would eat that shit up. The things this woman has seen, been through, legendary.

Looking over to Rylee, I give her a quick wink and smile. After the original Ranch was burned down, we helped Greta rebuild her dynasty. In return we took a ten-percent stake in it and the rest is history. It's one of the businesses I can truly stand behind with pride. It empowers and employs people of all genders and sexual orientation. And it gives them a safe place to conduct business while feeling free.

I'm so excited for Rylee, she has plenty of fresh ideas and plans that she has been implementing and testing out, all the while keeping the legacy in place. Everyone there loves her. They love Greta, but Rylee is bringing The Ranch into this century. It's such an exciting time. Fuck, if I didn't have this gig lined up or my slaughterhouse, I would have seriously considered working there. Maybe as an enforcer you hear about in Vegas, where they fuck shit up in the backroom and you never see the asshole again. I would have excelled at that job. But alas, here we are. Maybe I can offer my services on the side, I wonder if that would be frowned upon?

Dad interrupts my happy butterflies and rainbows thought with a snide comment directed to Greta. "Next, you can move out of my fucking house."

"Oh, I won't be leaving until you move my dead cold body from your side of the bed," Greta counters casually, waving dad off.

"I can arrange that tonight."

My mom jumps in to only make things more uncomfortable between the two. "I've always said that you two need to fuck your feelings out and move on. This sexual tension is becoming unbearable."

The room snickers, and Greta smiles then winks at my dad who is holding up his middle finger.

Once the commotion subsides, Papa asks, "Shall we continue?"

The rest of the room speaks, giving a brief overview of their operations, including drugs, politicians, law enforcement, academia, security and legal businesses; primarily all the places we launder our money through. Uncle Thomas clears his throat as he is the last to speak. After spending years under my dad learning the trade, we decided to put him in charge of information gathering because of how well he blends in. The guy was born with very generic exterior qualities, never sticking out. If we suspect a rat or hear rumblings of whispers and secret discussions, we send him in to gather the intel. Uncle Thomas has a small team under him for stakeouts, look-outs, and recon work, which includes Abi, our own version of a man of mystery.

With his hands in his pants pockets, leaning against the wall next to Greta, he speaks, "Sid was kind enough to handle the recent threat we caught."

I smile proudly, but I would do this shit for fun, regardless.

"Yes, and Blaise is handling the body," I add, no loose ends. My brother helps, when in the mood, with his version of information gathering and disposal.

Thomas nods in thanks before continuing. "We have our ear to the wall on a few other, minor things. If anything comes of it, you both will be first to know." Uncle Thomas has to be vague because only Papa and I know of the greater details, which are communicated in person at undisclosed locations each week or as needed if it's an emergency.

I assume this is why Abi was called out tonight, though we try to keep work out of the bedroom.

"Be sure to keep us apprised should it turn into something grander," Papa requests. Thomas nods once more, ending his update.

Sitting forward in his seat, Papa places his cigar in the ashtray and then takes a swig of his whiskey. The room watches him. "Great job, everyone. Thank you for your time this evening, and as the rest of this year progresses, you'll be reporting to my granddaughter more, not me. So get fucking use to it." And with those final words, the meeting concludes. We stay seated behind the desk and wait for the room to clear. My mom looks back at me, proudly, before following my dad out. Greta is last, with her blinged-out walker, Rogers following behind.

Still in awe of her every single day, I will never not believe, that woman is a fucking legend.

Following the closing of the front door, I rise and do the same with the office door. I trust our people but you can't help but have a nosey one in the bunch, hiding in the dark and lingering around in hopes of overhearing something they shouldn't.

It's human nature.

Papa opens the note I passed him, the one I found on Tash this evening.

Reading it out loud, he says, "*We see you when you're sleeping.*" He shakes his head. "Yeah, and we will see you too, motherfucker," he murmurs to himself.

"It was on the hood of my car this time."

He opens his desk drawer and places it on top of the others we've gotten over the past few weeks.

"Why is there blood on this one?" he questions, puzzled.

Blowing out a sigh, I'm not looking forward to delivering this news as I reveal, "It was stapled to Tash's dead, naked, and carved body."

His shoulders drop in disbelief. Leaning back, he rakes his tattooed fingers through his silver hair. "Fuck me."

"An upside-down cross was cut then cauterized on her torso." As I provide more details, his head continues to shake.

"This shit between your dad and brother needs to end, tonight!" he seethes. Blaise has been known to do things that are against the establishment, rebel against what we have built. The burned edges of the paper fit his MO. But leaving a dead body, carved, and the body belonging to Tash, it doesn't feel like him. But whomever it is has access to the estate, which gives me a small list to go off of, considering most are family.

Papa startles me, slamming his fists against the hardwood desk. "If this bullshit gets out, it's going to make us look like we can't keep our own fucking house in order. And if our members think that, then why would they stand by us as leaders?" His points are valid, I can't and won't argue them. And it makes me wonder, if it isn't my brother then who was able to casually walk through the gates with a dead body in hand? My mind races but my thoughts are quickly interrupted.

"She was our best fucking person to have in front of the pharma companies." Papa's eyes close, and his next words come out, exasperated. "I'll call them in the morning. Reassuring that nothing changes and, you, in the meantime, find someone comparable to Tash to get in front of them. We can't have them taking this as an opportunity to renegotiate."

I give a curt nod. "I will, Papa. Leave it with me," I reassure him. If anyone knows my brother best, it's me. And Papa is right, Blaise's resentment is going to start making us look weak.

And we are anything but that.

"I'll handle the body myself, don't call a cleanup crew," I advise, as it's less chatter that way. Papa ponders, then agrees. "Thanks, baby Sin." His voice is softer now. It's late and his eye bags are getting heavier.

"I can't wait for all this shit to be yours. I won't fucking miss it."

I laugh. "You will. I'll be getting calls daily from you, don't even try to deny it."

He laughs in response, smirking and shrugging his shoulders.

"Go home, sweet girl. Call if you need help, I'll make sure Tash's kid is taken care of. Placed in a good home with plenty of resources."

Smiling, I walk back over to him and bend slightly to kiss his cheek before whispering, "Thank you... and don't expect a call. I would hate to interrupt whatever Rylee has planned for you tonight." My tone is playful and suggestive.

"Why do you even think about that?" His face contorts, regretting the question. "Don't answer that, I don't want to know what runs through that mind of yours. Now, get going."

Laughing still, I skip out of his office cheerfully. "Night, you horny love birds," I shout into the rest of the house. Faint laughter from upstairs trickles down into my ears and I smile in satisfaction.

I have a strange need to push boundaries. I like it, it's fun and lightens the mood. Something we all need as I go home, tasked with burying a fellow member, and friend.

5

SID

Placing a cig between my cherry red lips, I flip my silver lighter and ignite a spark before putting the box back in the cuff of my white tee. Analyzing the situation before me, I mentally try to sort out how I'm going to handle Tash, who's still lying dead and naked on the hood of my Bentley.

"Sid, what are you doing?" My eyes light up, but not because I'm excited, because he cannot see what I'm doing.

"Daddy!" I chirp, careful to not draw suspicion as he casually saunters from across the street, where he, Mom, and Greta live.

Stepping away from the car, I meet him at the end of my driveway. His hands are in his pockets as he looks at me with disapproval. A girl smokes and gets judged, but if she is a cold-blooded killer, no one bats an eye. Society makes no fucking sense sometimes.

"Things are moving fast. Can you handle it?"

I suck back another delicious hit of nicotine then blow it out into the night sky. Keeping my eyes on the twinkling stars, I respond confidently, "I'll be fine. This," I pause holding my arms out, "is all I've ever known. We've been preparing for this my entire life."

"Yeah, well, your mom said preparing and actually doing are two different things." It's sweet. He isn't worried. But he's helping my mom feel better by checking on me. My daddy is the best man I know, and will ever know.

Lowering my gaze, I give him reassurance to take back to Mom. "I'll be okay. And I won't be alone. You'll still be by my side, same with Papa. Plus, we both have our vices, right? That shit always helps." I chuckle, thinking about the tunnel, my slaughterhouse.

"Don't let your brother fuck with you."

Smirking at his comment, I say, "Daddy, he won't. He only has fun doing that to you."

A loud sigh follows from my dad and I can feel his blood boiling. He and Blaise have a love-hate relationship, but it's fine. Growing pains. All families have them... I think.

Walking away, he grits, "I'll leave you to it then."

He's mad. But over the years, restraint has been learned and Blaise lives to see another day.

I watch and wait, not moving until I see him go back into the house.

Dropping my cig to the ground and stomping it out, I

head back to Tash. Glancing at her battered torso, I try to sort what the carved cross means. It's only part of our logo, why not do it all? And why does it have to be on my fucking car? Rolling my eyes, with my hands on my hips, dread hits. This is going to be a long fucking night. Scooping her up from under her arms, I drag her off the hood. Tash's mutilated body falls limp to the ground. Dragging her to the woods out back is the only option I have. I'm a tough bitch, but carrying a dead body lumberjack style that far isn't happening.

Hooking my arms under hers I begin our journey to the backwoods for a romantic evening together. Peering toward my parents' home once more, the dread is followed by guilt. I hate keeping secrets from him.

Only the devil knows what he would do if I didn't.

And I can't expect Mom to keep this from Dad either, as it's not fair to them, so I'll sacrifice and keep this knowledge and burden to myself for as long as fucking possible.

Tash's heels glide effortlessly along the thick grass as we allow the stars and moon to guide us to her final resting place. Looking down, dried blood stains her and she is absolutely stunning like this. I feel sweat begin to drip down my forehead, and I tilt my head back up so it doesn't slide into my eyes. My feet move faster across the yard and soon shadows of large trees begin to peer over us.

Twigs and dried leaves crack under my steps, and branches stick out, grazing my body as we maneuver throughout the thick brush. Taking a deep breath, fresh mountain air fills my lungs and my eyes close. *Home.* Nostalgia washes over me. I remember the first body my dad showed me how to bury in the back of Papa's woods all those years ago. The night was similar to tonight and I remember my heart racing with excitement, because finally I was old enough to learn.

The guy was a traitor, a pest. He deserved to die. And anyone who is against us is a pest who must be dealt with.

We broke into his home in the middle of the night. Walked down the long, narrow hallway of his double-wide before slowly opening his bedroom door so it wouldn't creak or alarm our sleeping victim. It felt like hours, but patience is important. Good things come to those who wait, and Dad was right, it did. Once we got in, everything moved so quickly. I jumped on the bed and straddled his waist with a knife in my hand. Dad slapped him once across the cheek so he would wake up. Missing your own death is a sin, obviously.

As the pest's eyes opened, I smiled down at him with excitement and sliced his throat from ear to ear. Warm, thick, red blood gushed out immediately, coating my hands and the sheets. The pest coughed a few times, splatter decorating my face and clothing. I felt so fucking alive.

Once he was dead, Dad leaned over, his baseball bat in the air, unused. "Baby Sin, congratulations."

That was my first solo kill and if you kill someone,

you've got to know how to clean up. Dad helped carry the body in plastic wrap, so as not to make a mess in his trunk. And together, in the woods at Papa's, we dug the hole and dumped him in an unmarked grave. The night smelt just like tonight, and my body relaxes, finding comfort in the memory.

I was eleven. It was my birthday.

We arrive at my spot, where I put others who matter from over the years. We are deep into the brush now, silence surrounding us with the odd hoot of an owl or the howl of a coyote echoing through the trees. Lowering Tash to the ground, gently, because she is one of us, and not a fucking pest like the others, my eyes roam the area until they see what I need. My shovel. It's leaning against the same tree I left it on, the sharp pick shining as the moonlight breaks through the thick leaf-filled branches, guiding me to what I need. More foliage crunch under my feet as I go to grab my tool, the cool metal a welcome relief to my already sore hands from dragging her body. Walking back to Tash, I notice her eyes are still open. A glint of light bounces off them as I bend down. Placing my free hand on her forehead, I brush it down over her eyes, pushing her lids closed.

Now she is at rest.

Blowing out a deep sigh, I rise and start digging. No point in prolonging it any further.

HOURS HAVE PASSED, I'm five feet into the ground, covered in dirt and excess sweat. My lungs huff deep breaths and my arms shake from exhaustion. Throwing my shovel over the edge, I brace myself next and pull my five-foot-two frame up. I could never dig the traditional six feet like my dad. I would end up stuck and likely dead after a few days.

Ironic, don't you think?

Kneeling next to Tash, I put both hands under her cold torso and roll her into her forever place. A loud thud follows and my face winces. "Sorry!"

Now, the painful process of filling the hole commences. But I found a quicker way than using a shovel. A large, long shop broom. And I just happened to have one next to where my shovel was. Grabbing it next, I start sweeping the dirt.

I figure it'll take half the time and will help my shaking arms rest, even just for a little while. My heart still races but I am determined to finish this tonight. Glancing up between sweeps, oranges and pinks start to fill the sky. Morning is upon us and my eyes instantly grow heavy. Adrenaline is wearing off, but I am nearly done.

As the last bit of earth finds its new home, then I drop the broom next to me and grip a bunch of wild flowers from next to my feet, placing them on top of Tash's grave. Wiping my forehead with the back of my hand, words start to flow out of me, in memory of our fallen.

"Tash, you were one of the coolest people I got to

meet and watch work. Truly a victim of circumstances, and I am so fucking sorry for that." Shaking my head, I slide my glasses back over my eyes. "I'm sorry you died on top of my car, though at least it was a Bentley, so it was kind of cute?" Looking down at the pile of compacted fresh earth, I admit this finally needs to be said out loud. "I was always jealous of your great tits, they always screamed 'welcome to Bozeman'. May you and the girls rest in peace... and enjoy your time in my woods. Please haunt those little fuckers who snuck in and did this to you." Looking around, I shout, "Yeah, you dumbasses, I see you!"

I don't, actually. But if they are lurking, I want them to think otherwise, because every part of me doesn't want to believe my brother did this. To leave creepy notes is one thing, but this body is a first and surely not the last. Then why torment me directly and not my dad, who he despises? Perhaps it's because I am about to take over, but so many people depend on us to provide for their families, he knows that. Fuck.

Looking down at the palm of my hand, the raised scar is a reminder of our bond, our promise. Everything points to Blaise, but my gut is screaming to not believe it.

Regardless, I'll always protect him until the day we both die.

Together.

6

SID

Morning has passed. The day is old and my bed is empty next to me.

Abi still hasn't returned from work.

I hear rustling next to me. Peering down, Jack and Sally are nudging my bed, telling me it's time to get up and feed them. My pretty babies, I could never deny them.

Bare feet touch the ground and the tiny prickly pig hairs brush against my legs. "Let's go, babies, time to eat." My words work them up further, cute snorts following as we leave the bedroom that I moved to the main level so my babies could stay with me at night and not have to worry about the stairs. Walking through the living room, the sound of their hoofs against the floor is like music to my ears.

My entire home is decorated in an abstract and unique aesthetic, as my mom would call it. The hardwood floors are black, which match the wood trim and cabinets in the kitchen. White quartz countertops are my pop of color to the place as the walls are lined with beautiful dark Victorian-style vintage wallpapers, yes, wallpapers, plural, because one style would be boring. I have dark blues and purples with blacks and dark creams. My furniture is a mix of velvets and corduroy materials, and my wooden fireplace mantel once housed many individual deep red candles. I have since let the wax melt, making a beautiful draped effect that could never be replaced or duplicated. From time to time, I add to it, placing my candles on top of baby doll heads to burn. The texture and contrast of it all turns my sensory neurons into override with happiness.

The kitchen tile, fixtures, knobs, and handles are all this beautiful vintage brass. My pussy clenches as I admire my castle. Fuck, this house gets me horny. The entire aesthetic is perfection combined with the different textures and patterns, and it tickles my brain in that special spot.

All the windows have brushed brass and iron designs integrated into the tinted glass, allowing me to wander my home as I please, not that clear glass would stop me.

Currently, I'm only wearing a black lace thong. Opening the back door, I walk into the yard, the clicking of hoofs and tiny snorts of excitement continuing to trail behind. Keeping a freezer outside filled with fresh body parts, I open the lid and grab an arm and leg of a guy we had to eliminate a few days ago. He was taking more than his cut when collecting from the dealers we allow to occupy our town. We, the heads of The Devil's Society, don't take kindly to thieves, among other things, therefore my father made an example of him for those who may have forgotten. We also have a no fentanyl, heroin, or meth rule. Shit's messy. We like to try and keep this place classy, which our pal was rumored to be trying to smuggle in.

Fucking idiot.

Daddy hung him proudly from the church. He was alive before his neck snapped when being pushed off the ledge, killing him a lot sooner than I would have liked. Before that, he suffered, though, his lips cut off and his hands removed. I'm not sure of the significance with the removal of his lips, other than Daddy being fixated on making them trophies as of late. He does something to harden them, then glues them on a small wooden plaque, adds a couple nails through the flesh around the lips, then displays them proudly on the wall outside of Greta's room.

As blood dripped and added more stains to the church steps, we would drive others by to show him off and, subtly, send a message: don't fuck with the hand that feeds you.

I smile at the memory of his limp limbs as I hold them in my hands.

Gus, my babies are going to love you.

Chucking the parts onto the lawn, Jack and Sally hustle over and begin devouring their dinner. After checking on the water dishes, I go back inside where the air conditioner is blasting. The heat is hot but the pigs need some fresh air. I have a muck pile where they can go to cool down, along with a shaded area, so they will be fine. My dad taught me everything I need to know about raising pigs and keeping them happy, and they are the pride and joy of my life.

Padding my feet along the floor, I rush to my library, which has shelves all the way to the ceiling filled with the most fun reads, splatterpunk to horror to history books, which teach me new tricks, like the mummifying tools I used on the pet in my slaughterhouse tunnel just yesterday.

Fuck, I can't believe all that happened only twenty-four hours ago.

In my library is my coveted scratched, vintage red gumball machine. I got this as a kid, and next to my pigs, this is another pride and joy of mine. Reaching into the bin beside it, I take a hold of a random Barbie and pull its head off. The popping of the head is satisfying, as I throw the body back into the bin. Unscrewing the lid at the top of the clear glass dome, I drop the head inside. It doesn't fall far, maybe a few inches, because she is filling up fast. I hope to get a new one soon!

For each kill, I add a doll head.

The pest from the slaughterhouse will always be remembered and celebrated in my home. And I guess, like my dad is doing with the lips, these are my trophies.

Tightening the top, realization washes over me. What

are we going to tell the others about Tash no longer being around?

Racing to my room, I find my Papa's contact and send a quick message,

BOSS BITCH

> Tash is resting. What do we tell the Archangels and Demons?

HELLHOUNDS WILL LIKELY BE curious as well, since Tash was in their ranks, but that's up to the Demons to communicate to them.

If you were to compare The Devil's Society to the Mafia, Papa and Rylee are like the heads or bosses of the family, with D and Cecilia, our Archangels, as the under-bosses. It continues down as such with Demons; Mom, Dad, Greta, Uncle Thomas, and others being similar to capos and The Damned being members waiting to be initiated. One major difference between the Mafia and us is, we are way fucking cooler.

BOSS MAN

> YOU will advise them on a story which contains some truth. Lies are easier to remember when a hint of truth is within.

> She's left to be with her family.

. . .

Fᴜᴄᴋ, no pressure at all.

We know her family is dead, it's why we took her in all those years ago, plus we saw her potential. He's right, it's the best message to send right now to not cause chaos and worry until we know more and have a plan on how to handle it.

BOSS BITCH

Understood.

Iᴛ's time to put my big girl panties on, but before I can, the doorbell rings. Rushing out from the library, I go to the door and open it, but no one is there. My nose scrunches in annoyance. Stepping back, I begin to close the door, but something on the step catches my eye, it's an old VHS tape with my name on it. My eyes squint, confused. Picking it up, I need to bring it inside before the heat gets an opportunity to melt it. Sending Rogers a message, he's going to kill me. He is within the ranks now, and rightfully so, but he is also my 'let me call my guy' guy.

BOSS BITCH

My cameras went down a couple of weeks ago. Oops!

THE REPLY IS PROMPT;

MY GUY ROGERS

Understood, Ms. Sid.

HE TRIED to call me Ms. Sinclair once and I threw up on his shoes. Absolutely not ever will I be referred to as something so formal. So he agreed to Ms. Sid after seeing the lengths of my dramatics. Rogers also doesn't lecture me like my Papa is itching to do. If I had the cameras working last night and all the nights prior when notes were left, we may know more than we do. It's no coincidence the notes started appearing around the same time the cameras died. I'm not a fucking idiot. It's all linked.

Focusing back to the tape, curiosity wins over coffee as I rush back to the main room. Before I can put the VHS into the player, the front door opens and I hear the latch clicking as it closes. My brows rise, concerned, as loud footsteps follow while I place the tape down on the table. Then the sweet voice of Abi follows. "Baby, where are you?"

My body relaxes and I rush to meet her. My arms wrap around her neck, ignoring the fact that her eyes look tired as I jump into her arms.

I cuddle into her warm embrace, I need this so fucking bad. The past day is catching up to me, as a loud sob escapes me followed by a river of tears.

My lips whisper against her skin. "I need you."

Her voice is calm and reassuring. "I'm home. I'm here. I'm so sorry I had to go, but I'm here now. You have me."

Inhaling her sweet scent, I'm taken aback slightly and she senses it.

"I showered before coming home. Last night was rough, messy, more than I anticipated. I didn't need you seeing that." Abi is always so considerate. She knows I'd worry if I saw remnants of her mission. I always want her safe.

Reaching to tease her skin with the sharp points of my nails, but I stop, remembering I had to snap them all off with my teeth last night while shoveling. So fucking annoying.

Instead, deciding to squeeze her harder. My bare breasts squish, pushing what cleavage I have up under her chin as I grind my hips against her waist. Grazing my teeth against her ear, I let a soft moan escape me and, immediately following, Abi's body shivers.

"I need you," I whimper once more.

The words that follow fill my body with joy. "You have me."

But I don't let her see that, reverting to the sexual tension building. "Take your pants off, I'm famished."

Abi's voice is hoarse with desire and her teeth bite her plump bottom lip. "Okay."

Untangling myself from her warm, comforting body, the tips of my toes touch the ground. My body aches from grave digging, but it doesn't stop me from kneeling before my fucking goddess.

I watch with hooded eyes as Abi's hands work frantically to undo her pants and slide them off, her panties follow, with a hint of wetness displayed.

"Aw, baby, you're a needy little bitch too, aren't you?" I tease while her head nods.

Inching my face forward, my nose traces mindless designs on her bare pussy, taking her scent of desperation and desire in.

Abi's hands sit lightly on my head, her nails scratching my scalp as her fingers get tangled in my hair. Chills drift down my spine, it feels so fucking good.

Unable to wait any longer, I need to get lost in her for a couple of minutes and forget about the life rotating rapidly around me. My tongue parts her lips. Abi's pussy is dripping already, her salty precum coats my taste buds, and I savor it, not swallowing until I absolutely have to. Finding her clit, my favorite thing, is when I allow her precum to trickle down my parched throat. She's already swollen, waiting for me to come play. Challenge accepted. She won't last two minutes before she's squirting all over my face.

My teeth pull at it, a loud hiss following, and her fingers grip my hair tighter.

The sting from my hair ignites my desire further, and I begin to fucking devour her. Lapping my tongue inside of her cunt, she wraps one leg over my shoulder, allowing me to get deeper. My hands grip her ass, and I pinch her skin between the sharp breaks of my nails. She moans loudly and I feel her body shift more. Looking up, Abi's head has fallen back. "You like that, baby? When it hurts?"

Her words are muffled by heavy breathing as I continue to eat my breakfast.

Moving back to her clit, my lips wrap around it, and I suck, hard. Abi's hips swivel as she begins to use my face to chase her release. My teeth tease her once more and her loud moans echo throughout the house. Pride washes over me, because I am doing this to her, making her feel this way, and I will never get tired of it.

I can feel her cum start to drip down my chin, but it's not good enough. Sucking even harder, I can feel her leg start to shake violently around me as she uses me to put her weight on because I know at any moment her other leg could go, leaving her a needy mess on the floor.

"Sid. Oh God, yes. Sid, please," she pants.

Don't worry, baby, I'm not stopping. Abi tenses before releasing a river down the front of my body. Her cum drips between my tits and down my stomach. I don't let up until I own every last drop. Spanking her ass, my hand cracks against her skin and she bucks against me once more before starting to settle down. I release her slowly from my mouth, kissing her lips gently. I praise, "Such a good girl for me." My eyes look back up slightly to find her mouth ajar and panting. I move back more and gingerly ease her leg off me, placing it on the ground, but I don't let go until I know she is stable.

"My mouth is way better than any fucking rose."

Abi erupts in laughter. "Yes, it is."

Kissing her pussy one more time before rising. I don't wipe my face or my body, instead letting the remnants of her orgasm coat my nearly naked form, proudly. Her fingers stay tangled in my hair, with Abi taller than me by a couple inches. Her eyes are still hooded, filled with desire, and her cheeks are bright red. Her dazed state is something I will never tire of seeing, she is so fucking cute like this.

This girl has me wrapped around her finger, because as these three words leave her mouth next, I melt, internally, and I know she is forever mine. "I love you."

That level of intimacy coming from my mouth makes me uncomfortable, but she knows how I feel, I always show her. So, instead, I tease, "I can't wait to use our new vibrating double-ended dildo later. We'll need new sheets once I'm done with you." Before Abi can respond, I wink and walk away, leaving her wanting more. I would use it on her now, but I have shit to handle first.

Hard work, then reward.

7

SID

Freshly showered with my hair in rabbit ear space buns, to pay homage to my family's history, and winged liner, I walk out of the closet in a black Elvira-inspired dress, where the sleeves are long and hang just off the shoulder, giving me a hot-as-fuck neckline. It clings to my frame and cinches even more at the waist and once it hits the knees, the fabric flares, leaving a beautiful train behind me. I splattered some red costume blood on my chest and face and kept the shoes simple, a black flat sandal that ties at the ankle. Checking myself out in the mirror one last time, I feel ready to go to Papa's and handle business.

My eyes move to the bed and they trace over Abi's body, which is covered by the thin sheets so rudely. She's passed out, exhausted from her night and our playtime. Her white hair is spread out over the dark pillow, it's angelic. I'm always so captivated by her beauty, she's classically beautiful, with minimal effort or care. And she doesn't need all that shit on her face to stand out, she stands out all on her own. Walking to the large windows which look out to the peaks of snow capped mountains and luscious green forests, I take the burgundy curtains and close them. I'm unsure when I'll be back, but this way the sun rising in the morning won't wake her before she is ready.

Grabbing the gold chain leashes off the hook on the wall, I leave Abi in peace, closing the door softly behind me. Walking to the back door, I call my babies in. "Jack, Sally. Let's go." Dangling the leashes, they jingle, further enticing them and it works. Snorts of excitement follow and I smile as I see their cute waddling bodies trotting toward me.

I latch the leash on each of them and bring them inside. We start toward the front door, but the black VHS tape and white label with my name on it catches my attention once more. I'm naturally a curious person, if I don't watch the tape now, it will drive me insane until I do. Hyper fixation will set in and all the *what could be on it?*' thoughts would only distract me while at Papa's.

Quickly, I give in, gripping it in my hand and the babies and I walk to the television, which has a VHS player attached; I don't trust modern technology, you never know who can be watching, listening and invading your thoughts without you even realizing it. The only reason I have a phone is for the society.

Sliding the tape in, the machine sucks it back and the

flapped door closes. I press play, then sit down on the couch.

The screen remains black for a few moments, then the screen glitches and faded bodies can faintly be seen through them. As the tape continues, the picture becomes more clear, and heavy panting plays through the speakers.

The fuck is my brother doing leaving me porn? This is so bizarre.

Pulling my phone out of the top of my dress, I send my brother a quick message;

> Why did you bring me porn? I didn't know we did that now.

I WAIT FOR A REPLY, but one doesn't come. Instead he leaves me on read.

Classic.

Sliding my phone back into my cleavage, my focus returns to the television. A grainy picture fills the frame before a red head appears. The camera is angled toward the girl, while laying on her back, her large breasts bouncing as she works the double-ended dildo into her cunt. The lady's partner has slid between her spread legs to join the party. Their pussies touch, their pelvises grind against one another's, and my nipples are rock fucking hard.

"Yes, baby," is moaned loudly through the room, and my pussy tingles with need. This is fucking hot. Squeezing my thighs together I continue enjoying the film my brother has graciously gifted me.

The sloppy sound of bodies slapping against each other is increased as the naked bodies continue to chase the release they desperately need. My own eyes become hooded and I seriously debate finger banging myself in front of my babies. A sin, in my opinion, but the devil is whispering in my ear, "Sinning can be so much fun."

While getting lost in my thoughts, another "Baby," greets my ears, and this time it takes me back. I completely sober up, alarmed.

I know that voice.

Leaning forward, my head tilts in front of the screen and my eyes squint.

The fuck?

Looking at the top right corner of the screen, it shows the date in small white text.

Last night.

The redhead then tilts her face toward the camera, like she knows it's there and grins.

This bitch.

It's that pest's sister! From my kill tunnel!

"Abi, baby, you feel so fucking good." Red's focus returns to her partner, sliding her fingers up her slender body. She squeezes her nipples then arches her back.

My face is turning red, I feel it burning up.

Rage is steadily beginning to brew in my loins.

Then, Red's partner tilts her head, I am still only able to see the back of it, as she raises Red's leg, and starts peppering her inner thigh with kisses.

Red's partner has bright white hair, this isn't making sense. And as Red sits up, she brings her hand forward and begins to play with her partner's clit.

The same clit I was sucking in my front entrance only hours ago.

I want to scream. I want to flip this fucking table then hang the traitor in my bed from her hair, killing her slowly while she's in the most excruciating pain. I want to embarrass her, put the whore on display, carve it into her forehead while shaming her publicly before she slowly fades away.

Red. Fire. Blood. Venom.

That's all I feel. That's all I see.

She's fucking dead!

Taking deep breaths in, I try to calm myself from being impulsive and reactionary. It's something I have been working on my entire fucking life. My babies sense something is off, they get closer to my legs, protective with the little hairs on their backs standing.

They know. And they are pissed.

"Don't worry, you'll get your piece too," I reassure them quietly while squeezing their chain leashes tightly in my hands.

Standing up, I quickly rewind the tape, turn the

volume up to max, and press play once more. Leaving the video on the television, I swallow my hurt as my lip quivers.

This is why I don't love. It hurts too fucking much.

A single tear escapes my hold, trailing down my face to my lips. I don't lick it, I let it stay living in the pain of heartache.

"Come on, babies, Mama needs her mama right now."

LETTING THE LEASHES GO, Jack and Sally make themselves at home as I shriek, "Mommy!" In the front entrance.

Heavy footsteps are first to make their way toward me. My body collapses to the floor. Lying on my side, I allow my emotions to rise to the surface. Tears fall from my eyes and a puddle of pain forms before me on the floor and pools against my cheek.

"Sid. What have I told you? Pigs outside," Dad gruffs in annoyance. "Jack, Sally, come out. Out." I hear the back door open, hoofs trotting followed by the door closing.

Whimpers escape me followed by a loud, uncontrollable sob. "Daddy. I need Mom. Where's my Mommy?"

Soft, hurried steps rush toward me. Kneeling down, mom's soft hand cups my face, "Hey, baby girl, talk to me. What happened?" Her voice is concerned, I never let them see me like this, if I can help it. Vulnerability makes me uncomfortable.

Tripping over my words, I stumble, uttering, "Ay..." My lungs fill and I scream, "She's evil!" I can't seem to get a coherent sentence out. "Traitor! Mommy, she's a fucking traitor."

Dad panics, "Sid. Speak. What the fuck happened?"

Glancing up at my dad, his face screams 'I don't know what to do.' It makes me smile whenever he tries to help me, even if he doesn't have a fucking clue what to do.

Swallowing the lump in my throat, I channel the brave Sid, the strong Sid. "Call Uncle Thomas. Put him on speaker."

Dad listens, not questioning me. Mom's face contorts with confusion. "Baby Sin, what's happening?" she murmurs while still comforting me on the ground. She joined me lying on the ground. Facing me, her thumb rubs circles on my face as the phone rings.

"Whatever it is, the answer is no, I don't have the energy today. I just had my dick sucked the hardest I've ever had it sucked by one of Greta's girls. I don't even think I can walk."

Mom and I burst into laughter by the unexpected greeting, meanwhile Dad's nostrils flare. "I can still take that machete away from you, you little shit. My kid heard that." And in that moment, I can feel Uncle Thomas's heart drop to the pit of his stomach.

"Hi, Uncle Thomas!" I try to cheerfully shout, but sorrow lingers and he knows me better than that.

"Sid. What's wrong?"

I pause, pondering how to phrase this without letting

them know anything. Tears well back into my eyes at the thought of it all, clearing my throat, I remind myself to be brave and ask, "Was Abi on a mission last night?"

His response is immediate. "No, I gave everyone the night off before the 'all hands on deck' meeting at your grandfather's."

I nod, absorbing it all. "Thank you! And please... don't mention this. And I'll keep your adventures my little secret too!" I giggle, trying to make light of my world crumbling around me. And my brother being at the forefront of it all.

Dad doesn't wait for him to reply, hanging up the phone as soon as I'm done speaking.

"Can someone please explain to me what in the ever-loving fuck is going on? Sid, baby, you get to eat pussy whenever you want. What is there to be sad about?" My eyes widen in shock. I can't believe he just said that to me.

"I'd eat your mom's pussy for breakfast, lunch, and dinner if she let me." He follows that boundary-breaking bomb with a wink to my mom, his soulmate.

Mom scolds him with the biggest grin adorning her face. "Elijah!" Then returning her focus to me, she says, "Aw, sweetie, your mascara is running all over your blood splatters."

Shrugging my shoulders, I bet it looks pretty and I reply, "It's fine. Let it." I blow out a sigh and deliver the news and end the suspense. "Uncle Thomas just confirmed it. Abi is cheating on me..." Pausing, I let them absorb this news as this is the first time I'm saying it out loud, making it real. "Last night. She said she had a job. Got a text and left. Then I saw things... so many things and I don't think it was the first time either."

Mom keeps rubbing my cheek. "I'm so sorry." She looks just as heartbroken as me. Abi has been in our family for years now, moving through the ranks from The Damned to Hellhound under Uncle Thomas, while also being directly under me at night. She's been my girlfriend for nearly two years. My first relationship and my last.

"Say the word. I'll do it. Anything for you, baby Sin." Dad's pissed, his skeleton face tattoo amplifies it, and if I didn't know him, I'd be shitting my pants in fear. He gets this black eye effect sometimes, and I worry this could provoke it.

Shaking my head, I say, "I'll handle it, Daddy."

His brow raises. "She's fucking out. That bitch is no longer trusted. Do you understand?"

I nod once.

I do. And I agree.

Then, at the worst possible fucking moment, my brother walks through the front door. Placing my hands flat on the ground, I push my body up, turn to face him and glare at Blaise fiercely. I would burn him, make him melt on the floor at my feet with my glare, if I could.

Resisting the urge, "Can someone grab my babies?"

Dad doesn't move, so Mom jumps to her feet and heads out back to get Jack and Sally, she senses the looming violence.

A deep snarl comes from me.

The many stages of grief have begun, and now I'm just pissed. Mom comes back with my pigs and I swipe the leashes from her hand.

Blaise is smiling, gloating even. As I walk by to leave with Jack and Sally, I mumble while passing him, "I hate you."

Dad is quick to hear my words and jumps to my defense. "What did you do?"

Smirking, I relish in the tension.

Mom instantly steps in. "Enough! She's just mad, hurt... broken. Sid, you don't mean it, do you?"

Shaking my head, I feel the mascara drying under my eyes. "I don't know what I mean anymore," I spit my words at him as I leave. He fucking knew. He fucking knew and that's how he decided to tell me? All I ever do is try to protect him, why? For the one time I need him, how could he not try and protect me back?

Greta must be awake from her nap, her walker echoes down from the hall. "I always hated that bitch."

I love this woman. Looking back, her face appears from behind the wall but Dad beats me to it. "Mind your business, old lady."

She laughs and snarks back, "Pussy is my business, asshole." Mom and I laugh hysterically because she isn't wrong. Well fucking played, Greta.

I take my family in once more before leaving. I am my father's daughter, but I cry, I feel, because Mom's blood runs thick through me too.

And because of them, I am Sid motherfucking Sinclair.

8

SID

Walking across the street to Papa's, I see *her* car is still in my driveway. Bitch better wake up and leave before her car is no more.

Jack and Sally snort, equally as disgusted as I am.

Oh dear, I guess we really are moving toward the anger stage. I'd cut that bitch right now and not blink an eye, then perhaps throw her body in her car and burn her alive.

How exciting!

My heart races at the idea, though this unexpected hit of adrenaline needs to calm down. It makes me have thoughts I can't have... yet.

First, I have shit to handle with Papa. A day in the life of a leader, I suppose. Oh, how priorities have changed, perhaps this is what maturing looks like.

Strolling up his driveway, I unleash the babies and lead them into his fenced backyard. My dad once had a body farm back here so they get excited and try truffling for hidden treats, if you know what I mean. The odd ear or finger still lingers beneath the soil, although I often wonder if my dad plants them back here for Jack and Sally to find.

Leaving them to it, I watch as their curly tails wiggle with excitement. As they start digging with their cute little noses, I go to the patio door which leads to Papa's office. Turning the warm metal handle, I find it unlocked. And walking in, I am greeted by his big smile, with hooded eyes from behind the large wooden desk.

I freeze.

What have I just walked in on? My absolute worst nightmare, no person should see any family in this state. Fuck me, well, I'm here now. This is happening.

Alarmed, my mouth opens and I can't stop it, "If I'm interrupting something, I can come back?"

Okay, that was polite, one point to me. But, internally I am praying and begging to Satan.

Please, Rylee, don't be under the desk. Please.

Papa rises and my eyes shift instantly to the wall. *Do not look directly at the light.* Clapping his hands, I'm startled and look back toward him. Fuck.

Wearing his classic gray sweats and white V-neck tee, his strong hands still clap. "No, you're right on time."

Releasing all the breath in my lungs, I sigh in relief. Rylee's not under the desk and Papa is completely flaccid. This is a win I needed today. "Thank you, Satan. I'll always be your humble servant," I sweetly say, speaking to the floor.

Papa laughs, shaking his head. "I don't even want to know."

Good, because I was not going to speak it out loud. But he was definitely day dreaming about something naughty.

Glancing back at him, I catch the moment when his face goes from cheerful and carefree to concerned and worried.

Papa's eyes take me in, catching every detail that the average person may not even notice. He has always been extremely observant. His thick brows scrunch and his lips pinch beneath his trimmed beard. "Speak. What happened?"

Biting my lip, I shake my head in defiance and brush him off completely. "I don't need to talk about it." Stepping forward, I can feel my skin warming, cheeks flushed as his eyes attempt to penetrate my soul for answers.

Yes, he is that fucking good.

Sitting on the soft brown leather couch, anxiety courses through my veins and my heart continues to race. I avoid eye contact and stare at his glass of whiskey and burning cigar instead.

I feel him move, his rings scraping against the hard wood desk tell me he is now leaning, still only focusing on me.

Papa knows this shit makes me uncomfortable, but he

doesn't give a fuck. Family is his priority, but I don't care to be that priority right now.

His tone is low, serious, and downright bone chilling. "Talk."

Closing my eyes, I try to muster the courage. Everything inside of me screams that he will be disappointed, and think I am an embarrassment. To be fooled by *her* would make our name a disgrace. The thought of it all causes tears to well in my eyes. Blinking rapidly, I force them away. What did that one movie always say, thou shall not pass? Neither will these tears.

Clearing his throat, Papa's approach changes, this time it's more warm, encouraging, and concerned. "Get out of your head, baby Sin. Talk to me, girl."

Leaning forward, I curl into myself, images of what I saw on the VHS flashing before my eyes. Shaking, I whisper, "I'm sorry."

"I need more than that. Nothing you could have done would make me disappointed in you. Have you met your father?" He chuckles to himself. I smirk, I mean, he isn't wrong. And he loves dad, so fucking much, but my dad can be a tad unhinged.

Sitting with that, my sadness and shame start to transition into pure fucking rage, because how dare she play me for a fool? I am a fucking Sinclair.

Spitting my words out, I reveal, "She's not with us. She is against us. Anyone who fucks a pest is forever an enemy."

Papa passes me his glass of whiskey, and says, "Tell me more."

Reaching out, I take his drink and down the amber liquid back in one go. It's fire on my throat going down and warms my cheeks further as I spit out the traitor whore's name for the last fucking time. "Abi."

Crossing his arms over his broad chest, Papa lets that marinate for a moment. "Baby Sin, I say this out of love, but fuck that bitch."

He's calm and I'm wondering if this is some sort of trick. Eyeing him up, I question, "What do you mean?"

"Fuck her. This is business now. Handle it." His bluntness catches me off guard, but he's right. The relationship is over, not only did she betray me but the entire society. Getting in bed with the enemy is the greatest sin, and she committed it... and because of her I have sinned too.

Still worried, drenched in shame, "You're not mad at me?"

Papa relaxes and walks toward me, placing his hand on my exposed shoulder, and squeezing it, he reassures me, "Never."

I needed to hear this so fucking bad, but I am finding it hard to believe it. "But I didn't even suspect anything. I feel like a failure."

"We all get played from time to time. What matters is how you get back up and never allow it to happen again, that's what people watch for in leaders." He pauses, allowing that to sink in before continuing, "Cheaters are experts in manipulation and gaslighting. Plus, this was your first real relationship, you were engulfed in the magic of it all. Fuck, I didn't even suspect anything, Sid. She played us all. You will learn from this and it will be the first and only time something like this happens."

As much as this stings so fucking bad, his words bring me comfort in an evening of self-loathing and pity. I can't believe I thought she could have been my forever, I'm so fucking stupid.

"So you're not going to take Diablo away from me?"

Chuckling, both his hands cup my face, forcing me to look him in the eyes. "No, you earned it, sweetie."

Grinning from ear to ear, I get excited. "So, can I kill her?"

"I would expect nothing less from you, baby Sin"

I don't know what I would ever do without this man. He has been a source of strength, comfort, and wisdom in my life. I'm the luckiest girl around to be able to spend quality time like this with her grandfather and to have such a strong bond with one another, there is no price tag on that.

"We do have some business to discuss, can you handle that?"

"Absolutely. Fuck that bitch, right, Papa?" He joins me in laughter while stepping back and returning to his chair.

"To be a leader, you cannot be nice, it's a weakness that if the wrong person sees, it will destroy your reign. They will walk right over you, Sid. Our team may be grown adults, but who doesn't like getting what they want when they want it?" He makes a valid point. He's repeated this several times to me, ensuring it's instilled in my brain. "It's about listening to your people, making them feel heard while also making firm decisions and sticking with them. Believe in yourself and they will believe in you."

"Understood."

"And I see them believing in you more and more each day. I think it's time. Five days from now, during the next full moon, because I know you're into that weird shit."

What a fucking day. This time, tears of joy stream down my face, followed by a sob of relief, "Thank you."

"Your biggest test coming into this will be how you handle Abi, the pest... then your brother." Fuck, don't I know it.

"Odds are good that Abi was feeding the pest information about our internal operations. Abi knew enough to provide a pretty good landscape to *them*."

Them being the loyalist to The Exiled, which died many moons ago, but like the pest from the tunnel, they just won't go away until I kill them all. One by one I will stomp on them, making their kind extinct.

We will always have a great relationship with the local MC, they have their businesses which we dabble in as well, aka arms and street drugs. Suppose you could call us associates of sorts. And we have a common enemy: anyone who tries to come in and take a piece of what we own. Key word here is try, because they never fucking win.

This is our town.

Tapping my chin, I ponder, until my phone interrupts my brainstorming session. Snatching it from between my breasts, looking at the screen I see it's Lucy, who helps keep The Damned in line. They can be little shits once initiated, their egos explode along with their overeagerness, which turns them into fucking idiots for a few months while she puts them back in their place.

"Ma'am, two of our Damned have expired. They were learning explosives and blew themselves up. Weren't paying attention to instructions, because apparently they know more than I do." Her words ooze with sarcasm and I fucking love it. It should also be mentioned that Lucy is a bomb and firearms expert, self-taught since a very young age, she could close her eyes and still shoot you in the middle of the forehead. She is a fucking blast, pun intended. I like her... a lot.

Rolling my eyes, I reply, "Bury them in unmarked graves. Not even the pigs will want to get within ten feet of their stupidity."

She snickers before composing herself quickly. "Understood." Then she disconnects the call.

Papa has the biggest smile on his face. "See. They respect you already. If you have gotten hers, you have them all. You were the first call she made, not me." Lucy is a Demon, therefore, calling to report the incident isn't unusual.

"Have you thought about Archangels? Will you keep

D on?" Cecilia also sat in that seat with D, but stepped back to focus on her family and raising the kids.

"For as long as he's willing."

He doesn't need to say it, I know he's pleased to hear my decision.

"You're brother, I'm worried. He's getting progressively worse, showing us what he can do with our own members." Referring to Tash who was nicely displayed on the hood of my Bentley, dead.

"Never in my lifetime did I imagine that the one person most capable of ruining everything we've built would be your brother."

"Me neither." I feel defeated, exhaustion from the day is beginning to wash over me. The high of learning from my initiation night has disappeared and I just want to sleep, to forget. "I'll handle it, I promise."

"Go home. Rest. Tomorrow is a new day."

Taking the hint, I fix my dress, and walk toward the patio door. Looking out the window, I find Jack and Sally instantly, thanks to the lighting in the backyard, and it appears they are occupied with feasting on a head. What the fuck?

Rushing outside, my feet move at new speeds I've never done before, as I shout, "Hey, no, babies! No touching," in an effort to deter them from enjoying the flesh any longer.

Once reaching them, I shoo them away with my hands and grab the head by gripping its stringy hair. Holding it up, the face looks familiar. Broken bloodied nose, bloodshot dead eyes, and the distinct odor of a pest. It's the bitch from the tunnel. A fucking cockroach. Someone's cut off her head and yet still, she continues to thrive, residing in my family's backyard.

"Babies, no. This bitch is vile. We don't eat vile bitches. I'll give you some more of Gus once we get home," I promise my now sulking pigs.

Looking at the cut made at the neck, it's just like Tash's cauterized marking.

"Blaise?" Papa startles me from behind.

Turning around, my eyes look the head over once more. "I think so, it has the same burns around the open cuts. And he said he would handle her after I was finished at the slaughterhouse, but I don't see a note."

He takes the head from me, shaking his own. "Go, rest. We can handle this in the morning."

Nodding in compliance and in no mood to object, I leash Jack and Sally and we head out.

What a fucking day.

WALKING HOME, it's dark, quiet, and uncomfortable.

Confused, my brain can't comprehend the head, my brother doesn't do body parts. Since he was a child, anytime Dad and I would prepare to dispose of bodies or distribute them to the pigs, he would leave when the chopping part started. His mind and body are drawn to fire, not knives, not blood, and not mutilation. This isn't adding up.

Leaving the videotape on my doorstep earlier today didn't help his cause, but ruling him out would be senseless. If, and that's a big if, Blaise is doing this, he is getting help.

But from whom?

Blaise was the only one I told about the pest in the tunnel, and he promised to handle it. This is what he deemed appropriate? Sneaking into Papa's yard undetected or without any alarms going off, and leaving that bitch for my pigs? It has to be him who left it.

I've always been so used to Blaise fucking with my dad, for as long as I can remember it has been an almost daily occurrence in life. But why fuck with me? I've always had his back, fucking always! Even after today, I still will defend and protect him... that is, after I'm done being pissed at him.

The tension with my dad and him has been building since the day he was born. A piece of it was jealousy, on my dad's behalf. Another man in my mom's life, Blaise never stood a chance.

He also didn't help his cause as time went on.

Blaise is quiet, observes, then attacks. He watched my dad, took notes on what made him tick, and then he would slowly pick away at it until Dad would react. Blaise plays the long game, he never fails, and he is predictable like that if you pay close enough attention.

Body parts aren't a long game, unless I'm missing something. I have to be.

And when Dad reacts, you could die. You don't fuck around with a man like him.

Mom would always do her best, rushing over to break it up when she could. Dad would get scolded, Blaise protected, and the hostility between them would build.

As time went on and we all got older, Mom realized the game Blaise was playing. It was from habit now, built into his daily routine. She would still try to stop them, but her fucks to give are slowly running out, and one day she will let them go at it until only one remains, I'm sure of it.

The bad blood is never going away, blood may be the only true solution.

As his big sister, I would attempt to convince my baby brother that he was delusional or reading into shit too much, but he's wise, seeing through my bullshit. Because that's what it was, I was spewing it to try and help Mom, because she would never speak of it but you could see it killed her.

Regardless of my bullshit, Blaise and I always had each other's backs growing up; we made blood oaths and promises. We are, or were, as tight as thieves. Even when the family started grooming me to take over for Papa at such a young age, Blaise always made sure I still enjoyed my childhood.

I remember how job shadowing days were always the hardest on me. It was intense, so much information and remembering of processes. I would come home exhausted and questioning myself; imposter syndrome is real. Blaise would sneak into my room and just hold me for as long as I needed him. We would spend hours just being, in silence while I wanted to scream. His calm calmed me, balanced me, and reassured me.

And now, I don't even know if I can trust him.

Walking up my driveway, I find the lying cunt whore's car is now gone, praise fucking be.

Leading Jack and Sally up to the front door, my heart drops. I immediately sober from my memories.

Another one.

Hanging before us is a torso, but not one I recognize. Reaching out, my fingers graze the skin, still warm. It's a fresh kill, fascinating, but who?

An upside-down cross is etched into the skin, the wound is cauterized, same as Tash, and a note is stapled into them.

Fear the unknown.

WELL, no shit.

Some people can be so fucking stupid.

Pulling at the piece of paper, staples fly and I slide the note down my top for safe keeping. Unlatching the pigs' leashes and opening the front door, I let the babies in before closing it quickly behind them. My hands move swiftly, removing my new friend from the door before my parents catch wind of it, my dad is forever wandering about at night.

The torso has rope tied around the waist, an iron stake keeps it hanging from just above my door frame. Assholes put a hole in my house.

Scratching my head, I truly have no idea who this body could belong to. Initiates, maybe? The Damned, but they would have small Devil's Society branding on them, and I don't detect anything of the sort on this person.

Unable to sort out who my new friend is, I decide to name the torso. Abi.

Oh, how I would fucking love this to be her.

"Come on, Abi, time to throw you in the trash where you fucking belong." An evil cackle follows and suddenly I'm not feeling so sad.

9

SID

The house smells of her.

Walking into my room, I flick the light on to find the sheets are a mess, tainted in love that never was. Aggressively, I throw them off the bed and race to the back patio door, tossing the evil energy outside, yelling, "Bitch be gone!" Damn that feels good.

Who needs therapy when you have this?

Smelling the evening mountain air, I decide I need, I crave, and deserve a night of cleansing. Pulling up the number to one of the local dealers, Winston, whose daddy farms some of our product locally for us, in the middle of his corn fields. But tonight I *need* something a little bit more numbing, freeing. Powder.

"Baby Sin, what do I owe the pleasure?" His deep husky voice sends chills down my spine. If I suddenly was into dick, he would be the first one I'd let in.

"I need some powder and a little bit of that grass your

daddy grows. Can you bring some over, Whinny?" I play cute to get my way, even if I know he would bend to my will regardless.

Chuckling at my antics, he responds, "I gotchu babe. Be there in a few."

Once he hangs up, I message the gate guards.

BOSS BITCH

Let Winston in once he arrives. Tell him to come to my office. Thanks!

THE REPLY IS IMMEDIATE.

FORTRESS PROTECTORS

As you wish, Ms. Sid.

FEET PAD up the dark wood floor staircase, leading me to the old master suite which I converted into my office. Flicking the switch, the beauty of my dark soul looks back at me. Like the rest of my home, the eclectic decor brings me almost as much pleasure as killing and my pigs. Mason jars of hearts, lungs, eyes, and brains submerged in some sort of clear liquid line the large wall of black shelves. Mom gave me these as a Christmas gift one year, all saved from my first kill.

Mixed between them are melted white wax candles, human skulls and framed retired antique tools from Mom's coveted collection. This room is full of sentimental memories and comfort. It's exactly where I need to be tonight.

The ceiling is decorated in torn black wallpaper exposing some of the cream paint beneath, adding depth to the space, and a vintage bronzed and crystal domed empire chandelier provides some light.

Thin, delicate fabrics drape from the walls, dark burgundies, blacks, and creams. In a couple of places, long, wide, gold-molded mirrors lean against the fabric. In here I am cut off from the outside world with the windows blocked. And it all makes me feel oddly safe. It's only me in here alone.

Before taking a seat on the couch, I pull my dress down and off my body, letting it fall at my feet. Stepping out of the fabric, I walk into the attached bathroom and throw on my black silk robe which hangs just above my knees. Tying it in a bow at my waist, I spin around and take in my appearance, the blood splatter and mascara stains remain. Throwing my hair into a high ponytail, I rummage through my drawers until I find what I need. Painting glitter glue under my eyes and overtop of my stained cheeks, my idea takes shape. Next I find my pixie dust. With just my fingertip I start placing it on top of the tacky glue. I work it all the way down to the corner of my lips where my lipstick is stained and smudged. At the same time I smirk to myself in the mirror, I hear the front door open.

"Up here," I shout to no response other than heavy feet coming up the stairs. My mind sobers from the chaotic thoughts. If it were Winston, why not announce himself?

Slowly I peek out of the bathroom entrance, my body jumps as a tall, broad-shouldered motherfucker wearing a cowboy hat and flannel shirt is smiling back at me. My glitter is everywhere from flying out of my hand.

Winston.

Slapping his chest, I yell, "You motherfucker!"

He erupts in laughter, thinking he's so fucking hilarious.

Slapping his chest, "Har har. Nearly gave me a stroke."

"Aw, I'm sorry, baby Sin. But, dang, don't you look all cute and mad anyways." he teases playfully, placing his hand over mine, which hasn't moved off him.

Winston is in his thirties and a classic fuckboy. He can look at a girl and her panties just melt away. Except for mine. His charm is cute, and Whinny is really hot, but my pussy doesn't ache for him.

Pulling back, crossing my arms over my chest, I pout, still sad about my glitter bomb of an explosion. "Did you bring it all?"

He winks. "Of course, boss lady. I'll always take care of you."

Rolling my eyes, I remind him, "Whinny, I'm not into dicks. You know this. Stop trying. I'm not a challenge you'll ever conquer, sweet boy."

He laughs hysterically then winks again, this fucking guy can't quit, "If you say so, baby Sin."

Total fuckboy move.

Reaching into his pocket, Winston pulls out my bag of goodies and I nod toward the large table in front of the couch. Walking over, he tosses it down and looks back over, but I cut him off before he can even start. "I don't need company tonight."

Sighing as if he is heartbroken, his face saddens, "Have a good night then," I swear that man can be as dramatic as me sometimes. Dark eyes glance at me, pouting and my head shakes, not giving in before he turns to leave.

Waiting until I hear the front door close, I step over my mess of pixie dust glitter and put my Miley record on, *Bangerz*, and start it on "Wrecking Ball". This song really resonates with me. Abi may have wrecked me, but soon I will wreck her.

Wheeling my gold frame with mirrored glass trolley, I bring it with me to the couch. It's decorated with cute knick knacks like white candle holders with dried blood dripping down the sides, wilted wild flowers, and vintage pearl necklaces draped over them. Reaching for the bottom row, I move the white and gold china teacups with black filigree painted on them to the side and bring the silver serving tray to my lap. It's mirrored but chipped and rusted, so I won't see myself looking back at me once playtime begins. Reaching for the baggy of fun which Winston left, I dump out the contents onto the tray, then place the tray onto the coffee table in front of me.

The fine white powder catches my attention first. *Cocaine, cocaine, takes away the pain,* I hum to myself.

It's in a small dime-sized bag. Opening the Ziplock, I dump it on the tray and lick the tip of my finger before sampling the product. Rubbing it on my gums, the numbness almost kicks in immediately. This shit's going to be fun.

Reaching for my silver letter opener and straw, which I always keep on my tray, I begin to cut and divide the coke before snorting it in quick succession up my nostril. It burns, and my eyes water, but it takes effect instantly. I feel so fucking alive!

My eyes shift and notice a gold frame with two smiling faces looking back at me. Except those smiling faces are nothing but fucking lies. Rising to my feet, my heart races and my face scowls. Walking toward the frame on my black glass desk, I grab it violently, and scream, "LIAR!" Before throwing it to the ground, glass shatters and the frame bounces off the floor. My feet move and stand on top of the shards, toes curling as I feel the jagged edges breaking through my flesh.

This bitch is going to pay. In blood, so much fucking blood.

The glass crunches as I walk off it, some still embedded inside of my feet. Bending over, I take another line, forgoing the weed altogether. Tonight is not a night to be mellow. Tonight I embrace all eighty-five sides of Sid Sinclair. I'm one dangerous bitch.

A sadistic laugh erupts from deep within.

Putting my phone on speaker, I call Greta. She's the only one who will understand me right now and what I need to begin to heal.

The phone rings and rings until a snarky, "What?" replaces the dial tone.

I waste no time getting to the point. "Take me to The Ranch."

"You know I can't drive."

Putting on my cute, 'I need a favor' voice, I respond, "Rogers! I know you can hear me. The Ranch. Please."

If they think they are hiding this love affair from me, they are wrong, and I love it.

Greta huffs, "You cheeky bitch. Fine. Be ready outside." She hangs up immediately, as if she's annoyed, but she loves our wild adventures.

Snorting one last line, I rush downstairs and head outside to wait for my ride.

Rebound sex is the first step in recovery.

THE RANCH WAS REBUILT on the same piece of land it originally stood on. Rylee's childhood swing was all that remained and is the only sentimental thing left on the property. Whenever I stop by with Greta, she gets nostalgic seeing it. I suppose it's also the only thing left of Nicole, her daughter who passed years ago at the hands of The Exiled.

Thankfully it's dark as we pull up to the large iron gates attached to a large stone wall that surrounds the place, along with multiple security guards. This place is more of a fortress than our family compound. The Ranch will never be destroyed by the hands of our enemies again.

Rogers nods, the guards acknowledge him, and the large doors to the promised land open. The driveway is short, with green hedges lining it and garden lights. A large three-story white cement castle greets us. When I say it's never burning down again, I mean it. Black cast-iron doors and window frames provide some contrast and match the black roof. With portholes and arched windows decorating the top floor, it almost looks medieval with a vintage Victorian flair. Rogers stops the car, meanwhile I lay in the back seat admiring the 'under the stars' effect he had put into the roof of his Rolls-Royce. I feel eyes on me, but I don't look toward them, instead, I simply admire and wait for the doors to unlock.

"You shouldn't be here in your state. You're about to be sworn in as their leader, the Diablo. And showing up grieving a lackluster pussy while pinned out on coke is not a good look," Greta lectures. When Dad isn't around, she can be rather responsible. How fucking annoying.

Side-eyeing her, I wonder, how did she know?

"Your pupils are blown, dear. I don't give a fuck what

you do on your own time but you shouldn't be out parading your state."

"I'm allowing myself one night of whatever this is. To get it out of my system so I can just fucking move on, Greta. Please don't lecture me right now." I'm slightly annoyed. Why bother bringing me if there was no intent on letting me enjoy it?

"You two stop bickering. I'll wait in here until you're done doing whatever it is we are doing here," Rogers interjects. He's a good man.

Tapping my chin with my finger, I question, "Wait, does my dad know about you two?" I had always suspected, but this is the first time I've been able to confirm their secret romance.

"The man is blind to anything sitting right in front of him. Doesn't suspect shit. And we will keep it that way," Greta barks. She isn't wrong, Dad is kind of oblivious to things like this. Her words are also a threat; she loves me, but she will have no issue punishing me if this secret romance gets out.

"Now that the lecture is over, can we go in, please? I need to play."

Popping the trunk, Rogers signals that it's go time. Sitting up, I escape the stars on the ceiling of his Rolls and welcome the sight of The Ranch. He grabs Greta's blinged-out walker from the trunk then opens her door, placing it before her. What a man, taking care of his lady.

Following her up the stairs and through the doors, white marble floors and a grand staircase greet us along with crisp white paint and walls decorated elegantly with art.

Faintly you can hear the soft sound of music playing, but audible moans overpower it from upstairs, carrying throughout the house. The corner of my mouth rises, that will be me as well in a few minutes when my pussy is being devoured.

Two hostesses come to welcome us wearing black dresses and matching black heels with red soles. Greta waves them off, but before we get too far, one speaks up. "Excuse me, miss, I think you're bleeding." Confused, we both look back and my footprints are clear in crimson across the floor, shards of glass still embedded.

"Shit. I'm so sorry," I apologize. Greta's face screams irritated. Oops.

"Fuck me, child. We will be in the living room. Have the nurse come to us," she barks at the sweet lady. The Ranch always has a nurse practitioner on-site, just in case, for precaution and to perform wellness exams or write prescriptions as needed, birth control being the primary one.

Greta mutters to herself as I continue to follow behind, embarrassed and immediately sobered. Guilt does that to a person and I no longer want to be here. How disappointing.

It's why I don't get high or drink. Impulsive thoughts always win and the regret and shame encompass me once I wake the next morning.

A bar is off to the side as we take a seat on the large

plush cream couch. I place my feet on the coffee table and the pain begins to make its way through my body, which is no longer numb. Looking over to Greta, I go to speak, but she stops me. "Don't say it. I don't need to hear it. I'm glad we came so we can get your fucking feet handled."

She always has had a way with words.

The nurse walks in with her medical bag, wearing blue scrubs, smiling. "It's too bad I don't have a foot fetish, Ms. Sinclair." I laugh at her corny joke. It's nice not having someone be so formal in your presence, refreshing.

Pulling up a footstool she takes a seat and examines my wounds. No words are spoken, no lecture given. Instead she grabs her tools and begins working.

Tweezers slowly pull out each broken fragment, followed by a cursed sting as she applies disinfectant. As one foot is finished, she wraps it in white gauze and medical tape, then moves on to the next. We sit in silence as I watch her delicately work on me. Some pieces are larger than the others, making my body cringe in discomfort. For a small frame, it sure did shatter nicely.

"I'll send you home with extra supplies. Clean it with warm water and soap twice a day, apply this ointment for the first three days only, and replace your bandages after every clean. I only want to see you again if they start oozing pus or the affected areas become red and painful. If you feel feverish, call me. All of these are signs of infection. Understood?"

I like a woman who is firm with me, so I smile, nodding, not wanting to disobey her. "Understood."

"Good. Now, go home and rest. I think you deserve some downtime." And she is taking care of me. Am I in love?

Greta slaps my arm, clearly aware of my inner monologue taking over.

"Thank you," I say graciously as the nurse rises, collecting her things and sliding the medical waste into its own baggy.

We follow her lead, rising as my feet throb in pain, but it's my fucking fault. I allow Greta to lead the way out to the main entrance. Before we are able to leave, instinct tells me to look up. And when I do, a familiar flushed face with hooded eyes looks back at me. And I am immediately obsessed with this new situation I have fallen into.

Lucy.

And she is doing the walk of shame. Yes, girl.

The moment she sees us, her hands cover her embarrassed face.

"Own it, Lucy. Nothing to be ashamed of," I holler at her playfully. Lucky bitch.

She giggles. "I'm not ashamed, I just didn't think I would have an audience afterward." Her face shifts from playful, to one of worry once she sees my bandages. But that doesn't change the reaction I have at seeing her. "Ice Cream" by Blackpink and Selena Gomez begins playing in my head, her movements slow and her dark hair mixed with pieces of blonde from her money shot fall around her delicate yet deceiving face, blowing perfectly in the wind I have created. Daintily, Lucy's feet go down each step, hand gently resting on the handrail with now narrowed eyes piercing into my soul.

A strong, powerful warrior princess is what she is, making my knees weak and my heart race even faster. Reaching the last step, Lucy walks toward me, asking, "Are you okay?"

Fuck, and she has compassion. My body wants to melt at her feet.

Before getting too caught up in my fantasy, I wave her off. "Perfectly fine, I stepped on glass." As if it's not a big deal, because it's not, to me, at least. Her eyes remain on me, but not judging my appearance or why I am even here. To a tourist or outsider, this entire 'I am Sid' vibe would be alarming, but not to those who know me, as they have always accepted me and my crazy.

"Get on outta here, Lucy. You'll only feed into her dramatics," Greta jokes, and we both laugh because she isn't wrong.

Lucy winks. "I'll see you around then." With that, she sashays ahead of us, but before disappearing, she looks back. "Call if you need anything. Oh, and ask for Ava, she is a fucking rock star."

I watch her disappear into the dark, captivated, until Greta shouts at me. "Get in the fucking car."

Bringing my focus back to the present, I see Rogers has both doors open for Great and me. Once in, they close behind us. Classy fucking ride. The star roof is shining bright, bringing a smile to my face. It's the little things sometimes. Briefly, I catch a glimpse of Rogers packing Greta's walker when a purple jewel reflects off the light. He is a good man. Not only for tonight, but always. He has always taken care of others, including Papa, for years before joining the society.

Once we are settled, Rogers puts the car in drive and takes off. The iron gates open and we enjoy the ride in silence, no questions, no conversation. Tonight has been strange, but also meant to be. I believe that everything happens how it should, even if we don't recognize it as it's all playing out. Greta's head is resting on the window, her breathing heavy as she sleeps during the journey home.

Looking up, I catch Rogers looking back at me through the rearview mirror. "I see all evil," he cryptically whispers.

I side-eye him in confusion, but then nod as if I understand the meaning of his words, playing along but absolutely clueless.

Pondering the cryptic message, my brother acts like he is evil.

Abi is.

And then sadness invades once more, this is why I'll never love.

10

SID

Days have passed. We are closer to my initiation than we are to my breakup.

Time heals all wounds.

This is true for my feet, but my rage and anger still live strongly inside of me, and it's all directed toward Abi and whoever keeps fucking with me.

Rolling out of bed, I see my babies sleeping peacefully in theirs. My phone buzzes on my nightstand. Peering over, it's the guys at the gate.

FORTRESS PROTECTORS

Abi is here for her things.

THE AUDACITY OF THIS BITCH. She's lucky I haven't burned everything, while hexing her soul.

BOSS BITCH

I'll be down with it shortly. Do not let her in.

ONCE I'VE REPLIED, I throw the phone on my bed so I can't hear any further buzzing. She can fucking wait.

Diseased bitch.

Every part of me wants to storm into my closet, cut her clothes up, then burn them in a box in front of her. But, petty Sid must take a back seat today, because I have other plans for this bitch. I mean, I can still put on a small show for the good folks, right?

Sliding on my oversized black band tee that hangs just below the knee, I add a pair of tall black leather boots even though I know they'll hurt my feet. It doesn't matter, because I am dressing for revenge. Looking in the full-length mirror, my hair is disheveled and my makeup from yesterday is a fucking mess, but it goes with my grunge vibe today, though it's still missing something. Rummaging through my accessories drawer I find exactly what I need. It's vintage, from the nineties, a black tattoo choker. Putting it on quickly, I take one last look at myself, loving myself right now.

Tugging her clothes off rather aggressively from all

the hangers, I hope they stretch in the process while I bunch them into a pile. I grab a few things she kept in the draws and add them to the mix, not caring how disorganized her things are. Once satisfied in the collection, I bend down, gathering it all into my arms. The smell of her no longer brings me pleasure, her scent is that of a rotting body on a warm day. I hate it. I hate her. The stench is strong enough to make me vomit.

Heels click against the wood floor and I use my elbow to push the latch on my door, then my hip to open it. The bright daylight shines down, warming my skin as I make my way proudly, down the private street to the large, guarded gate. Leaning against the hood of her car, arms crossed and wearing a scowl, the cunt waits.

The audacity, she has no fucking right to feel an ounce of anger, none. Petty Sid makes an appearance and I slow my pace, smiling in satisfaction. I hear the low chuckle of the guards, which only encourages my behavior. I knew I liked these bastards for a reason.

For the final fifty yards, I add a skip, a hop, to my step along with some humming, and the closer I get to Abi's nasty-ass face, the stronger her scowl becomes. Not only is she ugly on the inside, but the outside is directly reflecting it now. I was blinded by pussy and charm, but now I see her so clearly. Evil, she is pure evil.

"About fucking time," Abi mumbles, walking toward the gate. I release the bundle of clothes from my arms onto the warm, dirty cement road and step on them. Our eye contact doesn't break, my glare speaks all I care to say to her. She will not get the satisfaction of hearing my voice or giving a response to her ignorance.

No words will leave my mouth today, I am saving it for the slaughterhouse.

There is a slight gap between the road and bottom of the gate, the tip of my boot nudges the garments up to it, forcing Abi to bend over like a bitch, pull them through, and pick them up. I don't care if this takes all damn day, this, right now, is for me.

We get to a thick sweater, and Abi reaches, gripping the arm, and pulls with all her might, which isn't much, and it barely makes a dent. The bitch doesn't quit, though, pulling and pulling until her face turns red and sweat begins to bead on her brow, how embarrassing. I know she wants to walk away but pride won't allow it.

A pair of hands clap behind me and my head turns to find my brother. I'm thrilled he has come out to support me. Looking back at Abi, she's let go of the sweater and has risen to her feet.

"Little brother, so glad you could make it." My face remains neutral, but my mind is confused, why did she call him that?

Abi taunts, "He knew. The entire fucking time, he knew." My heart drops, my breathing hitches, and I bite the inside of my cheek to keep my face from reacting.

"We were in some cabin we found abandoned in the woods. Kasey, the redhead, was eating me out and as I was about to cum, my eyes locked with his through the window.

He didn't move, he stayed watching as my orgasm rippled through me." Her brows move, encouraging a reaction from either of us, but if this is a game of chicken, I'm winning.

Her petite hands wrap around the thick bars of the front gate, her pathetic face peering through the gaps, and do fuck I wish she was in jail, and those were the bars to her cell.

"Blaise, you got off to it too, didn't you?"

Please, brother, do not take the bait, I plead internally, hoping he can feel it.

His feet crunch against the loose gravel, his footsteps stopping as he arrives next to me, placing his arm around my shoulders in solidarity. I am so fucking pissed, but we will not show weaknesses in public.

Abi's voice becomes husky. "Did you touch your dick while thinking about me? I got you so fucking hard, didn't I? It's why each time we were in the cabin you would watch, isn't it?"

Please, brother, keep biting your tongue.

Gently Blaise squeezes my shoulder in reassurance while Abi continues her taunting.

"It's a shame you found out when you did. I wasn't quite done with you and your precious little club." It's the last thing she says before turning around and speeding off in her vehicle.

Once she is out of sight, I throw my brother's arm off me. "You fucking knew? The entire time?" I shout, it's a mixture of rage and hurt. How dare he?

"This is why I didn't tell you, I knew you would get pissed." He is such a man.

My entire being shakes uncontrollably. "I knew you left the tape. It was your writing on the label," I spit, adding, "I'm your sister. We bled for each other. We promised each other. Fuck with Dad, sure. But me? How could you?" I look down at my scarred palm, where a single line rises from scar tissue from the oath we made to each other years ago as kids. Does it mean anything to him anymore? Is he so lost that he has forgotten?

"I know…" He pauses as my words finally sink in, knowing he's wrong. "Fuck. Sometimes the shit with Dad bleeds over to you. I'm sorry, sister." His face drops, he is genuinely ashamed.

There's one more thing I need to fucking know, my words are hushed so he can only hear. "Were the bodies you?"

He looks back up at me confused. "What bodies?"

"Tash's on my car the other night, cauterized and carved? The limbs from the pest at the Slaughterhouse, you said you would take care of? And the notes with burnt edges?"

Blaise's head shakes slowly. "No, I swear it. Not me. I promise."

I nod my head as my mind races. "If I find out you're lying, keeping secrets from me again after protecting you, you are dead to me, understand? I will not stop him from hurting you. Dead to me, dead to the world." My words are harsh, but truthful. He's hurt me deeply and I can't allow it to happen again. I need to protect myself, my heart, and my family, including my found family. The Devil's Society.

"You fucking knew this bitch was hurting your sister and you just watched?" Shit. It's Dad.

"Get out of here," I urge my brother, but he never backs down from a challenge with our dad.

Looking up the street, Dad is marching toward us with his baseball bat in hand, pointing it at my brother. "You have crossed the fucking line, turning your back on family is un-fucking-forgivable."

Blaise looks at me like a deer in the headlights. "How did he know?"

I nod toward the guards and he grabs the roots of his hair. "Fuck!"

Through gritted teeth so my dad doesn't see, I say it once more. "Get out of here." And he does. Spinning around quickly, Blaise races through the guard stand and out the other side and into the thick brush.

"PUSSY!" Dad shouts, standing in the middle of the road. "Sid, come by later, your mom will want to see you," he states before turning on his heel and walking back home. Dad knows all about violence and protecting his family, not comfort. And as much as they hate each other, my dad would protect my brother in a heartbeat if needed.

I look at the guards who are acting like they are minding their business, and hiss, "Traitors."

A bunch of, "Sorry, miss," follow, so I decide to

remind them, "You may as well start calling me Diablo. Get used to it, fuckers. Initiation is coming." The threat is subtle, but they get it.

Leaving the clothing on the ground, they can clean that shit up, I begin to skip back home, hoping my brother is going to be okay. To the left of me, I hear someone in the bushes. "Psst, Ms. Sid." It stops me in my tracks. Turning my head, Rogers's face pokes out and I nearly erupt in laughter. Before I can, he puts his finger to his lips and nods for me to follow him, and I do. I trust Rogers with my life along with Jack's and Sally's, and that level of trust is indescribable.

"Rogers, I am not in the right shoes for a hike," I whisper playfully, but I also very much mean it.

"We are going to the security room inside your grandfather's, don't worry, Ms. Sid."

Why couldn't he just text me to meet him there? I mean, this is kind of cool, stealth mode and all, as it helps keep my day interesting. Well played, Rogers.

Creeping through the shrubs and foliage, we reach the end and step out onto my Papa's driveway and make our way inside through the side entrance, which is closer to the security area this way. Rogers is a master of information gathering online and through the connections he has built throughout the years. I admire him tremendously.

Stepping inside, he enters a code onto the control panel and a retinal scanner scans his eyes before the door unlocks. Opening it, we are welcomed by a dozen screens, all split into four frames, each capturing every inch of our town, and the compound.

"Please take a seat." I do as I continue to scan each screen. Rogers clicks away on some buttons and an image of my house takes up the monitor before me. This sneaky bastard, he knew I would be irresponsible when it came to getting shit fixed.

"I had backup cameras installed around your property, Ms. Sid. I knew you wanted to be responsible for your own security on your property, but not having extra precautions in place would have kept me up at night," he explains.

I place my hand on top of his and reassure Rogers that I'm not upset, I am grateful. "Thank you."

"I found a note in your grandfather's office, burnt ends with threats of unease." That's one way of putting it. "It had me curious, Ms. Sid." His other hand presses the space bar on the keyboard, and a clear video plays from the night I found Tash, causing my jaw to drop, horrified.

"It wasn't your brother, look."

Oh my fucking god.

I pull up my phone and dial the person I know who can help me, and as they answer, I say four simple but powerful words when coming from a Sinclair. "I need a favor."

11

ELIJAH

"You'll have to come home eventually, your mom will miss you." I'm not beneath using Rain to get this little fucker back here. My kid hasn't lived with us for years, and his mother thought it would be best if we built him his own place within the family compound. As his home was being built, Blaise moved into a rental in town and never left. None of us liked him outside of these walls, but the kid's skull is as thick as this bat, and I knew he wasn't going to listen.

Calling his phone again, it goes straight to voicemail. "I'll fucking cut you off. You'll have no money and no house outside our walls. You will have to move back here, you remember, right? It's the house you refuse to fucking live in because you are an ungrateful shit." Throwing the phone, it bounces off the couch and I can feel my body filling with anger. Since the one time with Rain, many years ago, my kid has been the only one capable of bringing me to the brink of a complete rage-induced blackout.

"What now?" Rain, who is very annoyed, asks. The tension within our family makes her feel things other than happiness, and that's what gets to me the most. But once Blaise and I get going, we don't stop, pushing each other's buttons to the maximum in order to watch the other explode.

"He knew that diseased cunt was cheating on our kid. He would watch her. He fucking recorded it and left the VHS for Sid to find," I seethe in disgust. If you can't trust your family, who can you trust? Then again, our family history isn't one to reference in this instant.

We killed my cousin, then my uncle. And this was all after I made my mom burn herself alive, and we fucked over Rain's birth father's dead body... Because we killed him too.

Rain's hands cover her face, she can't speak but her head shakes.

Walking up to my beautiful girl, I bring my lips close to her ear, and whisper, "I'm fixing it." And this time, she doesn't stop me.

Whether or not I do what I am implying, that is still up in the air, but to not plead with me to stop makes me feel like this could be a test. It's too good to be true. My eyes shift, though I don't question it, and instead, I slowly step backward, reaching for my baseball bat, which is leaning against the island, and leave.

Once outside, I howl into the sky, "Daddy is coming to play!"

Before I am able to get into the Range, I see my dad standing at the edge of his driveway, looking over at me. "If you kill him, it may be the one thing you regret, son." Dad is always full of wisdom and shit, but I work on impulse and instinct. I nod, letting him know I heard but will not listen. Because my kid is going to regret the day he was ever born.

PULLING UP TO THE RENTAL, it's a townhouse just off Main Street. It's an average-looking three-story narrow townhouse. I called Thomas on the drive over, and he's now standing on the sidewalk in a pair of shorts, slide-on sandals, and a black tee holding his machete. He knows better than to meet me without it.

Getting out of the Range, Thomas nervously questions, "Boss. What are we doing here?"

"Ah, Tommy boy! What a beautiful day to be alive, isn't it?" I say sarcastically. And I hope to fuck he doesn't answer.

His eyes widen nervously, a brow arches, and he takes one step backward. I watch him closely then laugh into the sky. Motherfucker thinks I'm going to kill him.

Fuck yes, I still got it.

Walking closer to him, I narrow my eyes, rub my tongue against my sharp, exposed fangs, and then tilt my head. I stop just as our toes meet, my bat spinning. It's like I'm ready to hit a home fucking run. I then whisper, "My son. Not you, dumbass."

With a trembling breath, a sigh of relief washes over my protégé. "This is as good of an idea as your dead body mushroom growing business, boss." Thomas sarcastically loves to rub that one in my face. No one wanted to eat my mushrooms that I grew off dead bodies at the farm. However, I did. I ate mushrooms for weeks until I couldn't stand them anymore.

Then Dad fucking insisted on the body farm being removed once summer was in full bloom. Apparently flesh rotting from defrosting was not something he wanted to look at every day while in his office. By the time I finally got around to removing our new pals, Brad's eyes had begun to melt out of his droopy face. I kept the eyes, and I hide them in Greta's room when I get bored and wait for her to notice them and freak the fuck out. The worst time was when I glued them to her bathroom mirror, at her eye level. Rain cut me off from the sweet well that is her pussy for three days. I nearly died.

"My son has been a very bad boy for a very long time. And I've had about enough of his shit."

"Wow. I know you two have had your differences, but he's your blood."

Now he understands how serious I am.

"Exactly. And he betrayed his blood. It's time he learns the consequences of his actions."

Walking past Thomas and up the paved path, I lift my boot-clad foot and kick in the door. "Daddy's here!" I shout into the townhouse.

I wait for a response, or any commotion, but silence greets me. I nod my head, and Thomas moves in front of me. "If you see him, capture and restrain," I instruct.

Rushing up the stairs, two at a time, I dent the drywall with my bat the entire way up.

"You can't hide from me, motherfucker," I taunt, hoping to coax him out. But it doesn't seem to work. Pussy.

I check the bedrooms, closets, and bathrooms, then head to the third level. Opening the attic latch, stairs slide down and I crawl up them. Turning on the flashlight on my phone, I examine the hot dry space full of insulation and dust. No Blaise.

Letting out a monstrous roar, I wonder, where is he?

"He isn't here," Thomas so obviously points out, shouting from the main level.

Shouting back down, I give further instructions, "Destroy the place. Everything. He fucked with my kid and your next Diablo." I pause, could someone be hiding him from me?

"If we find out someone is aiding him, burn them down and destroy everything they love. And bring me *him* alive. He's mine!"

"Understood," Thomas responds between the loud crashing of dishes falling to the floor. I start with the attic stairs, completely tearing them off their hinges, then throwing them through the wall. Next, I storm into his bedroom. His bed is the first thing to catch my eye.

Jumping on top of it, I whip my dick out and piss on it. A large yellow wet spot begins to form, thus destroying his sheets, mattress, and box spring. Once done, I shake off and tuck myself back in. Adding a couple holes in the drywall with my bat, I push his dresser over before heading downstairs to Thomas, who I catch mid-slash to a pillow with his machete.

"Well done, Tommy boy!" He's never been one to disappoint me, and consistent reassurance, helps keep it that way. He smiles, finishing slashing the pillow before turning to face me with the biggest grin on his face.

"Thank you."

Confused, I question, "For what?"

"This. Letting out my stresses or frustration on this house. It feels so fucking good."

Placing my hand on his shoulder, I squeeze it. "Everything I do, I do it for you."

Thomas's eyes well with tears and I am now incredibly uncomfortable. Emotions are Rain's department, not mine. Reaching for my phone, I call her immediately and put it on speaker. I hear her pick up, but I'm able to interject before she says anything.

"He's going to cry."

Rain laughs. "Thomas. You okay, buddy?"

He sniffles, whipping his nose. "Elijah said... Everything he does is for me. And it's about the nicest thing I have ever heard him say to me."

I burst out laughing as Rain mumbles, "You motherfucker." She knows exactly what I've done.

"Thomas, he heard this song playing one day and uses that line on people. He did it to Sid first, then me. We all slowly caught on. It's his go-to phrase if he wants to fuck with you and make you feel good. Remember... Elijah is an asshole. That will never change." She speaks to him the entire time like he is in first grade, making this even more funny to me. Rain then begins to reassure him with some concern. "In his own way, he cares about you, but you know he would never get deep, right, Thomas?"

His face is red, fist clenched, and his machete falls to his feet.

Thomas is going to clock me.

Relaxing my face, I wait for the impact but instead he gets me right in the balls. A loud yelp escapes me as I fall to the ground. The phone beats me down and my bat rolls alongside of me. Rain is howling on the other end and through squinted eyes, I see Thomas smirking.

Through gritted teeth and stinging balls, I rasp, "I'm killing you next." Even though I am wildly impressed with the balls on this guy for following through with what he just did to me.

"No, you're not. He is your only friend," Rain retorts through the phone, then she adds quickly before hanging up, "Thomas, you better get out of there before he can stand. Bye, boys."

He takes her advice, snatching his machete then leaving me in a state of pathetic misery. They did me a favor, as it's only giving me more time to plot my traitor of a kid's death. Slow, painful, and full of cries and screams.

Blaise is not a Sinclair. The name no longer wants him, and neither do we.

12

SID

The oil barrel burns bright with red and orange flames dancing out of it. All the evil that once lingered in my home is dead. Bad omens are removed and solace is returning to my sanctuary. A sanctuary which has a killer fucking playlist. Brody Dalle's "Don't Mess with Me" plays loudly in my ears as I dance around warm flames in black fitted slacks and a black high-neckline long-sleeved shirt, paired with a black harness with gold accents and a belt. A pair of combat boots adorn my feet while I have the time of my fucking life; my feet are still bandaged and hurt like a fucker, but fashion comes first.

Jack and Sally watch from the patio where they are lounging, gnawing on a couple ears from the freezer, basking in the full moon's energy alongside my crystal collection.

I feel renewed, ready for fucking anything, like my initiation.

Papa said I would receive *the* call, and once I'm provided the location, I would have only an hour to arrive. I'm excited to leave the past behind and begin my future. I also am desperate to speak to my brother, who I hope shows up this evening.

Betrayal or not, he is still blood. And the anticipation of this evening is killing me. Anxious about the unknown that this evening brings, but excited to experience it all.

Looking down at my palm, at the scar he and I share, my heart aches. As pissed off as I am with him, I still need him. We shared an oath, a promise to one another. No matter what, we are always here for one another and when one takes their last breath, so will the other. It's very Romeo and Juliet, it's very dramatic, and it's very us. Naturally, until death and after was my idea. We were out in the yard, deep within the woods exploring.

I was twelve, he was ten. My training to become Diablo had started a couple of years prior, but he kept me grounded and reminded me how important it was to continue experiencing life as a kid, even though many aspects were infiltrated with very adult situations. I liked it, the experiences and training. I never fought it, but he was right, I needed to try and achieve a balance of both worlds while I could.

After exploring the woods for hours that evening, we found a place to rest and just exist, the two of us, the only two people in the world, or at least that's what it felt like at the time. Pulling out my knife, I started playing with it between my fingers when Blaise snatched it from me.

Instinct said not to get mad, so I didn't. Instead my eyes met his and I knew he had other plans for us. His face screamed mischief and mine begged him to take me along for the ride.

Waiting, I watched then followed his lead, cutting my palm in a single straight line like his. We brought our hands together and let each other's blood run through us, solidifying our bond, our promise. I felt a surge of energy blast through me in that moment, as our eyes remained looking into one another's soul, and he spoke two simple words, "For life."

I added, "Even in death. No one without the other." Blaise nodded, agreeing before we separated, letting the warm blood trickle down our wrists and arms.

It was after that night, the fighting with Dad and Blaise really amplified. He became more outspoken and I don't think either of our parents enjoyed the idea of the blood bond pact we had made that evening. Mom was more understanding and tried to protect my brother, but sometimes he would dig such a fucking hole for himself it made it impossible.

Even though he was younger, Blaise would often speak up for me when I didn't do it for myself.

To be clear, I didn't need him to do this, and most of the time I was completely unaware and would be initially pissed off that he had. I was grateful for the opportunity and didn't want anyone thinking otherwise, but he was adamant.

I learned so much from my brother growing up, he taught me to always be myself without apologies or regret.

We have one life, and we must live it.

And I do, each fucking day, for myself, for him, and for those who can't. Take me as I am or fuck off. I have always had the confidence and self-acceptance, but as lines blurred between my childhood and adult life, he helped ensure I kept all sides of me intact.

For a kid he was so fucking wise, he absolutely got his soulful side from Mom. His short temper and not giving a fuck is all Dad. I like to think I am a cute version of both our parents, a little crazy mixed with curiosity and a little heart, it makes for an exciting time.

Turns out my little heart is a lot of heart, internally, because I feel so fucking deeply, others' energies can impact me dearly. Mom calls me an empath. Other people's energies tell me if they are good or bad, which is why doubt riddled my body after Abi, because my senses failed me with her, where it had never failed me before. And as confident as I am, self-doubt can try and over-power my positive thinking.

Lying in bed at night, sometimes my mind still beats me up for that one. I try to remember that it's okay, but it's not always that easy. Recharging and protecting my peace is also top priority, if negativity is around me for too long, it becomes too draining.

Which then leads me to killing them or burning the evil out of this fucking place, like tonight. That vile cheating cunt tainted my sanctuary.

My focus returns to the beautiful flames before me, enchanted by their meaning and significance, until my phone vibrates in my pocket.

Taking my headphones off, I snatch it and see it's Uncle Thomas. This fucking guy is in so much trouble, I chuckle to myself as I answer, "I heard you kicked Dad in the balls and lived to tell the tale of it," I joke, he laughs in response.

"I don't know what came over me, but after I realized I had, I nearly shit my pants out of fear."

I burst out in laughter and ask, "Are you still hiding from him?"

"Fuck yes, I am terrified." His laughter is no more, instead it has quickly turned into worry, poor guy. Dad will absolutely seek revenge but he won't kill the guy, I don't think.

Changing the subject, I have to know, "Have you seen my brother? I'm worried."

A soft sigh exhales on the other end. "I'm sorry, baby Sin, I haven't. What happened? Your dad is really mad, it's the first time I have been genuinely worried for Blaise."

A tear pricks my eye. "He knew some terrible things and kept it from me... until dropping off a VHS exposing it all. I was so hurt, broken even..." I pause, gathering my thoughts before rambling on because my other thoughts about Blaise are no longer relevant since

Rogers showed me the true evil among us. "You know how Dad gets if I cry." It's the only explanation I need to give.

Uncle Thomas immediately understands. "I think that teacher from your middle school can attest to that."

Dad chopped off the hand of my seventh-grade teacher, Mr. Donald.

He knew kids were picking on me, I told him several times, and he did nothing. Secretly, I think he liked watching a young girl having her lunches stolen, or shoe laces cut off her sneakers and seeing nasty notes taped to her back.

Misogynist.

Eventually it got to me when Mom asked how my day was and a river poured out of my eyes.

That night, Mr. Donald's hand was in a box gifted to me from Dad, his body fed to the pigs, and the kids got mail a few days after Mr. Donald's disappearance. Individually bagged teeth with a note saying, *You're next*. I never had an issue with bullying again after that and no one has made me cry since, until now.

It's a combination of Abi and Blaise that made my heart shatter. I will always hate Abi. Blaise is temporary, but try telling that to Dad. Like I said, this is years of buildup coming to a blow.

"Anyways, that's not why I'm calling. The favor, I got it. Are you ready?" Uncle Thomas asks, as a giant smile adorns my face, making it past my eyes and to my brows.

I squeal in excitement. "Uncle Thomas, you are the

best uncle ever!" My babies start snorting, my happiness is contagious.

Regaining composure, I think, fuck, I need to do this tonight. A fresh start under the full moon. "Can you give me an hour then come to the slaughterhouse with it?" Squeezing my eyes shut, I try to telepathically tell Papa not to call yet. *Please, this needs to be done in order and properly.* Fuck, I hope he hears my wishes and allows me this.

Uncle Thomas interrupts my telepathy mission. "You got it, baby Sin."

I smile, excited. "Okay, I need to get ready. See you then," is all I say before hanging up.

Be gone, all evil. You are not welcome here.

AFTER QUICKLY PUTTING out the fire, I grabbed all the extra supplies I had been dreaming of since *everything* came to light and changed my clothes. Fuck rainbows and butterflies, I desire rib cutters and skull chisels. A manic laugh releases and fills my Bentley. Most of my equipment is at the slaughterhouse, but this is a special kill which deserves special items from my personal archives.

My babies stayed home, so I will message my mom to bring them to initiation once we get the notice. Looking in the rearview, I am so used to seeing their cute faces looking back at me. My lips, painted in dried blood-colored lipstick, pout, missing them.

The roads are quiet, it's well past midnight, and driving through the town is peaceful before the chaos. A part of me hopes to catch a glimpse of my brother, so I can pick him up and protect him. To return the gesture of the years of him protecting me. Now that I know the truth, I kick myself for ever thinking he was the bad guy in all of this. But my mind spiraled and nothing screamed out to not question his allegiance and loyalties.

My leg shakes with anxiety, it's gone past the point of anything I ever expected and I fear I cannot save him. The sharp points of my black press-on nails dance along the steering wheel. "Please, Blaise, let me see you," I softly speak to myself as my eyes look down each dark alleyway I pass. "Where are you, baby brother?"

This is all my fault, but there's nothing I can do now other than try and fix it, try and help him.

Pleads ignored, I reach the edge of town and catch no glimpse of him. Bright lights of the town dim behind me and I am brought back into the darkness of the wild. It then occurs to me, he will likely miss my initiation. "Fuck." We were supposed to do this together, and now I must go alone.

Silence is running through my brain and I hate it. Turning on some music, "Breakin' Dishes" by another queen of mine, Rihanna. The beats bring me back. I am badass, I am Sid fucking Sinclair. I run a slaughterhouse and don't give two shits about what people think of me.

As confident as I am, I have moments of doubt and

sadness, and that's okay. Because I am about to break some motherfucking dishes up in here.

Turning on my blinker, I pull into the gravel side road. My accessories piled into the car rattle as the car shakes while crunching over the gravel.

"I swear if this road ruins my hair, I will cut a bitch… Oh wait, that's already the plan." Smirking to myself, my headlights shine on my tunnel and the gravel turns into pavement as I pull up into it. Typically I park outside, but I have shit to unload and I am not dragging it all behind me.

Sweating in this getup is not happening.

Pulling up to my spot, the long metal chain sparkles from the reflection of my headlights. Uncle Thomas isn't here yet, which pleases me, as it gives me extra time to set up the entire scene.

This is an event. Not a detail will be missed or compromised.

Parking my Bentley, I keep it running so I have enough lighting and my beats on to keep me moving. Hopping out, I catch a reflection of myself on the side of the car and take the opportunity to do a quick fit check. My feet, still decorated in white bandages, and bare legs, and reaching my thighs, white ruffled and torn tulle greets my eyes, a white lace strapless bodice wraps around my torso, and my long dark hair hangs in waves over my shoulders and down my back. With dried blood red lipstick on my lips, I added my mother's signature broken doll cracks on my cheeks and forehead with dark eye makeup. Lastly, the tulle veil, it's very eighties and I am obsessed with the dramatics of the entire piece.

Bright lights shine on me, breaking my focus. It can only be one person. Turning my head, I look toward the oncoming vehicle just as "Kill This Love" plays next. Fucking perfect.

Smiling, my teeth show and the fang toppers pinch my lip, because I wanted a piece of Dad with me here too.

The vehicle stops, and the man of the hour hops out. Uncle Thomas.

"Where do you want her?"

Giddy with excitement, and as much as I want her set up for the scene now, we have things to do first.

Rubbing my hands together, I reply, "Help me move this shit first. The traitor can wait a little longer."

13

SID

Car lights are off, and white candles decorate the area as I sit on a red blanket covered in red and black roses. The flickering flames leave shadows dancing on the cement cylinder walls as Uncle Thomas brings the last item out for my audience. Abi.

Everything is set up, waiting for our guest of honor's arrival. Thrown over his broad shoulders, her legs hang tied at the ankles and her body is limp. We have replaced the chains from my last visitor to hooks. Uncle Thomas hoists her up, throwing her shackled wrists on either side of the hook, holding her in place as her feet dangle. He slaps her hard, only once, to wake her. The crack of skin echoes, bringing a smile to my face. Today is a good day.

"Thank you," is all I say as he walks back into the darkness.

He waves me off, "See you later," and I know exactly what he is referencing. His vehicle starts, the engine purrs before roaring to life as he reverses swiftly away, lights still off to not ruin the moment.

Taking a long stem rose in between my fingers, the thorns are sharp as the pads of my fingers dance along the tip of one. Abi's eyes slowly open, dry coughs follow, then realization washes over her face. Her jaw drops, the self-declared untouchable being has been touched and brought to me for her last day.

"Did you have fun playing your games?" I artfully ask, the question is calculated. Will the truth fly off her tongue or must I force it out of her?

Her voice is growly as she whimpers, "Water."

Uh, absolutely not.

"Wrong answer. Try again, please." Because I am not one to be rude, obviously.

Abi coughs once more. "Help."

My nose turns. Gross. How pathetic.

Bringing the rose to my mouth, I stick my tongue out and press the sharp green thorn into it. It stings, but only for a brief moment, then all I feel is warmth running down my chin. I leave my tongue hanging and as I slowly rise to my feet on the soft blanket, blood begins to trickle down my cleavage and stains the white lace. It's perfect.

Dropping the rose, it falls next to me as I step forward. Taking the steel folding ladder, which is leaning against the cement wall, I unfold it and place it near the pest, because that is what she is now, a no name, worthless pest.

Carefully my toes curl around each cool step, her eyes

watch my every move and I push my fang into the hole on my tongue to ensure my blood is still freely flowing. When I reach the top step, allowing me to look down on her, the dripping blood falls into her open, dry mouth.

She closes it promptly,

"Good girl, drink it up." Because this is all the mercy she is going to get from me.

Choking, the pest spits it out, and it splatters on my lace dress. How fucking rude.

Stepping down swiftly, I throw the ladder off to the side, and it hits the rocks, crashing loudly in our ears.

"I try to help and that's the thanks I get?" I am disgusted, but not surprised. Ungrateful bitch.

"Did you think I would never find out? Did you have fun playing your fucking games?" I ask rhetorically, because if she answers she is dumber than I thought.

"I hated you the entire fucking time," Pest speaks like her words will sting. They don't. I'm rid of her evil and I welcome all the fun we are about to have together.

Licking my lips, I allow the blood coating my tongue to decorate my face, before responding to her ridiculous statement. Rolling my eyes, I clarify, "No, silly, I mean framing my brother."

My declaration silences her gagging and coughing.

"Rogers sees all evil. And he likes sharing his visions with me." Walking up to her, my feet pad against the cool rubble. Gripping her jaw with my fingers, I press my sharp nails into her skin. "And you are one evil fucking bitch." As predicted, she wastes no time spitting on my face. Her dramatics are petty and pathetic, whereas mine are exciting and fun.

Annoyed, I press my nails harder, piercing her skin, but I don't stop. I push harder, breaching her cheek deeper. Wetness collects on my hand from her tears, loud whimpers of distress follow, and that's when I realize I forgot to put on my music to tune this annoyance out.

I penetrate her mouth then quickly pull my nail out before she can bite me, the catty cunt.

Stepping back, I continue, "The notes were clever. I have to admit you had me and my Papa fooled. The timing was impeccable, you knew my brother was acting out more against my dad and took advantage. Well fucking played. And taking the last pest from my tunnel, leaving pieces around Papa's yard for my pigs. Clever, but telling. Because the one thing you didn't take into account was Rogers. He has impeccable security in place for when, at times, I fail to maintain mine, which you also knew. You knew I couldn't be bothered to fix my property's cameras, but you didn't know others would have my back. Amateur." When he showed me the footage, it all made sense, how she has full fucking access to the compound and not once did I even suspect her.

Her response fascinates me. "I don't fucking care. It worked. Your brother is a dead man walking. Daddy thinks he has been a very bad, bad boy, doesn't he?" I suspected she would be disappointed in her flawed plan and being found out, but she's pleased, gloating, and sadly she's not wrong. Interesting.

I sense she may have a few more surprises up her sleeve. Typically, they beg for help, apologize, and cry at this point. But not her. Interesting, indeed. What more do you have to share with the class?

"You are so fucking stupid." Her voice is hoarse as blood continues to drip out of her mouth, and with a sadistic smile, she continues, "She screamed as we burned her wounds. Tash was alive when we cut that cross into her stomach. Passed out just as we finished cauterizing the wounds. What a shame, she missed her own death." This bitch.

"And her brand, for The Devil's Society?" I question.

She chuckles, throwing her head back. "Alive. Made her watch by tilting her head up. I understand why you like doing this shit so much."

Cutting her off, I say, "No you don't get to relate to me, so nice fucking try." There is one thing I need to know, though, before I begin playing. "Why?"

Coughing more, Pest shakes her head with a smug look on her face that I want to chop off. "You have no idea who I am, do you?"

My head tilts. *Perhaps not, please tell me more*, I talk to myself, not audibly responding to her question. I wait in silence, patiently.

Closing her mouth, she swallows some of the thick blood building in her mouth. Exhaling heavily, she pushes some of it out of her nostrils, laughing like a hyena. "I wanted to destroy you. Your family and the fucking society. Burn you from the inside out, and I have. You're out hunting each other."

Walking to the table behind me, where my tools are beautifully displayed, I pick up my bone saw. This bitch is getting annoying with her cryptic messages.

"This was my mother's," I explain, holding it out in front of me. "A prized possession from the archives. And I cannot wait to use it on you." I bounce with glee on the balls of my feet.

Looking back up, I focus in on her shoulders. At any moment, they will exhaust from being hung in this position and pop right out of her sockets. I would rather draw out that pain for her and go straight for her feet, but that would be too easy.

Perhaps a Father's Day gift is in order, her lips.

Blowing out a sigh of frustration, because why did I have to throw my ladder, but swallowing my pride, I skip to where it landed and fetch it back, setting it up next to my pest. If her rambles don't turn into useful information, I am done listening to her nonsense. Reaching forward, I am about to grip her lips together and use this giant saw for fun on something so dainty, but she stops me.

Her muffled words take a moment to register, and my head turns, taken aback by it all. My saw drops to the ground. "Dalton was my dad." I release her mouth and she continues, smiling, "I waited and waited and finally got the fucking revenge my family deserves. I broke you. I broke your dad, brother, and made your grandfather even doubt his blood. I. Fucking. Won."

My heart drops and my mind races. What the fuck?

How? Does Dad know? There's no way, because he would have kept an eye on them and handled it as necessary. This changes everything, but at the same time perhaps nothing at all, if she is unable to live to tell the tale.

Cutting off my rampant thoughts, her annoying voice penetrates my ears, catching my attention once more. "Mom was a random hookup after he took over as king of The Exiled, the only group I recognize. She found out about her pregnancy after your family fucking slaughtered him. Then hung him from the church, massacred, for days on display," she screams with hate.

Oh, the bitch is mad.

My brows rise and I whistle. Yikes.

I change direction, ripping her shirt off with my bare hands, exposing her bare breasts, where her brand is. Rushing down the ladder, I grab my handheld kitchen torch, in honor of my brother, and race back to her. Flicking it on, I press hard on the release button and boil her skin.

How dare she wear our brand, our mark, our legacy.

Pest screams and a bit of blood from her mouth lands on my hands, but it's drying now. What a shame.

She tries moving her body away from the heat, twisting and turning, but I only follow her moves. Smiling in satisfaction, I understand why both my dad and Blaise are drawn to this method. Mom once told me Dad took a flamethrower to a bunch of people in a cult her birth father started, then Dad would tell me my favorite comfort story about how he had his mom burn herself alive in a giant fire off the coast of North Carolina. Dad used intimidation, forcing ol' Granny to take every step backward into her own death. It's how my parents met, because their parents got married and Mom's dad turned out to be a crazy fucking cult leader, could you imagine?

Blaise will spend hours diligently burning people and corpses, and it calms him, the flames, the heat, watching the skin contort and melt and bones turn into dust. It's fascinating when you think about it.

I fucking love my family.

Focusing back on the bitch, no evidence of the brand remains, only burnt and boiled skin. Letting go of the button, the flame stops and I turn the gas off, whispering, "This is only the beginning of our fun together."

Moans of pain continue to leave her. "You look fucking stupid." She tries to take a dig at me mid-scream, but I roll my eyes. I couldn't give a shit.

Tossing the torch back to the table, I grab a scalpel this time. I don't care to listen to her speak any further. Plus, this ladder is getting annoying, the pitfall of being short, I suppose.

Squeezing her lips between my fingers, I take the sharp medical grade scalpel and pierce her skin before I start slicing around her lips. I go deep, ensuring the cut is clean for display. Pest tries to shake me off by moving her head, but it doesn't work. This isn't my first time. Stupid bitch.

Once freed, I toss them behind me to collect before I leave.

Blood is now gushing out from the incision, covering her white teeth and pouring down her exposed and burnt chest.

Giggling to myself, I think it's time for my next surprise. But before I can set it up, my phone rings. Who the fuck would call me right now? I wonder, completely forgetting initiation could happen at any moment. Rushing to it, I answer. It's Dad. I skip all formalities because I am fucking busy. "Is this important?"

"Where are you? Your car is gone," he questions, and I roll my eyes.

"At my slaughterhouse, and you are ruining the moment. I have to go."

Pulling the phone away from my ear, I go to hang up, when I hear, "I'll come by."

Huffing out a breath, I plead, "Not this time. Please." I need this, it's closure for me and the family. Closure he doesn't even know he needs. And I would like to keep it that way until I'm done and can speak to him in person.

Dad pauses, so I look at the phone thinking he has hung up and ignored me, but then he responds, "Fuck, fine. But know I'm really fucking bored and your mother will have to tolerate the consequences of that," before hanging up. That was easier than I thought, thankfully. Almost too easy, but I won't question it.

Placing my phone down the front of my top, I continue setting up my showstopper, something I found antiquing years ago and never thought I would get the opportunity to use, until now.

The Judas cradle.

The one I found is made of metal, though some are made of wood.

It sits on four legs, reinforced in the middle for stability and weight, and topped with a beautiful, shiny, sharp pyramid as a seat.

I position it under her bottom, the top pushing slightly into the fabric of her pants and helping the hooks at her hands hold her up. She shakes violently, her words slurred. "No, no, no,"

I think she means, *yes, yes, yes*, because this is absolutely happening.

One, two, three, you're going to die bitch.

I smile to myself at the fun mantra I've just created.

Once satisfied with the positioning on the Judas Cradle, I find my phone in my top and click the sacred red button the IT guys installed. The red button controls a levy system I had constructed, which lowers our friend here, placing all her weight onto the sharp pyramid top, the lower I drop her. I watch the slow process with great excitement. Fuck, music. Scrolling through my playlist, I find the most iconic song for this moment, "10 Things I Hate About You" by Leah Kate. Pressing play, the guitar starts, my head bobs, and then it starts to pick up. Screaming along with the chorus, I hop around the screaming bitch before me. At one point I change the words and shout, "Daddy issues."

Circling her back, the point is well implanted into her rectum, destroying her internal organs. I smile as blood begins to stain down her white pant legs, because who wears fucking white? Stopping, I look down at myself and laugh at being dressed in head-to-toe white. But I want her bloodstains, it's a badge of honor, something I will wear with pride all night long, then put it into storage should I ever want to remember this night.

Reaching her front side, I notice her eyes are now bloodshot, and more crimson flows uncontrollably from her mouth down her exposed torso, but it's not enough. I need more.

Finding my bejeweled gas mask, I slide it on over my face and snatch my rib cutters and decide it's time to play.

Typically, this tool is used on the ribs, hence the name, but not today. No, I need more blood, more pain, more body parts to take home with me. Clicking the red button on my phone once more stops her from lowering any further. Uncomfortable, her hips wiggle and heels fidget against the dirt. Still tied at the ankles, and tightly contained on all ends, I inform her, "Sweetie, this is how you're going to die. Nothing is going to get you out of this predicament. Now, please, stay fucking still."

More cries from the desperate pest echo around us

and I am so fucking over it. Tossing my phone back in my top, my work here is not yet done.

Stepping forward, I brave her teeth and stick my fingers inside her wide-open mouth. Gripping her slippery, lying, horrible-at-oral tongue, I swiftly move in with my rib cutters and cut the muscle in one, clean slice. More blood splatters, the majority of it landing on my mask and chest.

My head tilts as she begins choking on herself, and soon her lungs and stomach will drown from ingesting too much of her own blood. Stepping back just in time, she vomits on herself. Lifting my mask, I look at her in disgust. "Show some class, would you?" Her eyes seem like they could explode out of her head at any moment, but it doesn't deter from the fact that I hate fucking vomit. It stinks and really is the grossest shit to clean up.

Annoyed, I scurry around and reach for the hooks. Unlatching her cuffs, I watch in slow motion as her body falls backward. Her pelvis remains elevated and she now resembles a human version of a pyramid.

Smiling, I pick up the bone saw I dropped some time ago and place my mask back on over my face. I must keep my makeup somewhat fresh for later, after all. Bubbles form at the pest's mouth. She's choking, but not fast enough for my liking.

Placing the saw between her teeth, I stare into her eyes and cut. At first, it's easy, just skin, then the resistance greets me, her jaw hinge, and I apply more pressure. Placing my bandaged foot on her forehead to keep her steady, I continue, noting the progress I've made as the bottom part of her jaw starts slacking to the side. My hands are covered, dripping in warm, thick life, life which is draining from her rapidly. My saw reaches her ear, cue for me to angle down and continue my cut, completely removing the bottom portion. This part is a tad thicker, but I've never met an adversary I couldn't beat.

At some point she stops struggling, her body becoming slack and her jaw now fallen to my feet. Dropping the saw, I lift my mask and hands in victory. Because I always fucking win. I always get what I want and nothing can ever get in my way.

My chest heaves, catching my breath from the intense arm workout I just did, then my phone vibrates against my heart. What timing. Blowing my hair out of my face, I pull my phone out of the top of my dress and see it's Papa. Opening the message, it's a pin to the location. It's go time.

Looking down at the liar, I'm almost positive she's dead. If not, she will be very soon, between the pain up her ass and the lack of face with a side of burnt flesh, the odds are stacked against her.

Skipping to my car, I look back at her once more, waving. "Bye, bitch, I have a party to attend."

14

SID

Cars surround the open meadow.

Mountains keep us private from the outside world. This moment is ours.

A small fire is lit, rocks encompass it and thirteen shadows stand around the dancing light, accompanied by two sweet baby pigs, Jack and Sally.

Taking a deep breath, I hold it in my lungs, trying to slow the racing of my heart. My palms are damp and moths flutter in my stomach.

Closing my eyes, I exhale slowly through my nose. Repeating this process a couple more times assists in elevating my heart rate to a somewhat acceptable beat, followed by picturing Jack and Sally frolicking together. They always calm me and provide me with the most joy a human could ever experience, besides killing.

Raising my hands, my fingers tangle themselves in my hair, where my veil dramatically hangs. Unclipping it, I let it fall out of my hair because tonight it's being replaced with a crown.

Before gathering the courage to get out of the Bentley, I reach for the visor and flip it down. Sliding the small cover, the mirror reveals itself with the automatic lights. I take in my appearance: blood is dried under my chin to down my neck and beyond, and the splatter on my face really adds to the aesthetic. I like it. What a night, a bloodied bride, a corpse in her slaughterhouse, and next to be crowned queen. My life is surreal but so fucking perfect... Almost.

There should be fourteen around the flames. Closing the visor, I shake my head and rid myself of any sorrow or negative thoughts. Tonight has been perfect and I will not bring any bad energy with me to this.

Opening the car door, I step onto the crisp grass, which tickles my toes, and breathe in, filling my lungs with fresh mountain air. A gentle breeze blows delicately over me as I take in the moon's energy. Slow steps follow and my feet guide me toward my family, chosen and blood. I don't focus on them, my eyes and memory are trying to absorb every ounce of this moment, to ingrain it into my brain for life. This is not a moment to be forgotten, this is girl fucking power at its finest.

Silence greets me once I reach the cluster of members waiting for me. All of them are in black, from head to toe. The contrast of our outfits makes me smirk, it's perfect. Reaching forward I attempt to take a hold of the leashes for my babies, but Mom shakes her head once, denying me. I nod, understanding, and turn my attention to Papa who is standing at the twelve directly across from me.

"So let it begin." His deep voice brings chills up my spine and down my arms.

Standing still, I am unsure what is to come next, or if I am expected to do something. I feel my chest rising, hyper aware of all my body's movements and the movements of those surrounding us, uncertainty will do that. The others step back, including my babies, each of them give a snort, cheering me on.

This has been the first time I have been so nervous and intimidated in my life. But I am a strong motherfucker, nerves and anxiety will not deny me of that.

"It is your birthright, your destiny, and my honor to name you the next Diablo of The Devil's Society. It has been the greatest privilege of my life, watching you blossom into the leader you are today." Papa pauses. I can feel his emotion and pride and I swear to fuck if he makes me cry, I will be so annoyed. The urge to stomp my foot is strong, but I resist out of respect for the process.

"This is the first ceremony of such stature we have had. I racked my brain for days, months even, trying to decide how this should be done. Then Rylee reminded me, sometimes the best solutions are the easiest. And she was right, as usual." A few chuckle. I can see Papa's distinguished smile lines embedded into the depths of his face, shadowing against the bright flames. I admire how much he loves her, Rylee, a love like Mom and Dad's. It comes once in a lifetime and you never take advantage of it.

As the group silences, he continues. "When it's your turn to pass this responsibility down, you will do it as you see fit, which I predict will include a lot of enthusiasm, calculated chaos, and extravagance." That's a nice way of him saying dramatics, as no expense is too dramatic, and in true me style, of course.

"Sid, please take a seat," he instructs. My face contorts in confusion. Does he mean on the ground? But my questions are quickly answered once he steps aside, revealing a wooden high-back throne, and I burst out laughing in disbelief, because I will not cry. This gesture is beyond purposeful. This is love. A bond, a respect between grandfather and granddaughter, and a leader and his heir. Unable to help myself, I turn into a blubbering idiot, tears I have been holding back flooding my cheeks as my nose sniffles trying to mask my emotions. But I am not ashamed, I let them flow.

My toes curl as grass tickles between them, and I ground myself once more before preparing to take the first step toward the rest of my life. In my periphery, I catch a glimpse of Greta, Lucy, and Uncle Thomas as I pass them. Greta's distinct aroma of nicotine and musk invade my nose, which then brings me to think of her and Rogers as a couple. It occupies my mind, distracting me until reaching the throne.

My hands reach out and touch the hard, wooden arms. I shake my head in disbelief. All of this for me? Are they sure? Papa reads my mind, placing his hand on top of mine, and he curls his fingers underneath and gives me a gentle squeeze of reassurance while whispering, "Take a seat. It's yours now." Dammit, this man is attacking me in all the feels tonight. Well fucking played, Papa, well fucking played.

Once his hand releases from mine, I turn around and let the wood guide me down. Bending my knees, I lower myself until my bottom reaches the hard surface. Closing my eyes, I take another deep inhale through my nose. The tears have subsided, but could resume their flow at any moment, it seems.

"It was many years ago when we, the upper ranks, started to notice The Devil's Society emblem being carved into the skin of The Damned, our new initiates, and to those who joined us prior to that." My eyes shift, unsure of where this could be going. "What you all didn't know was, us old-timers did it first." The corner of my lip rises, curious and excited about where this could be going. Have they had them this entire time?

Papa undoes the first buttons of his shirt, pulling one corner to the side. He steps forward so I can see. I lean forward, but all I see is his silver chest hair. Looking up at him, I ask, "What am I meant to be looking at?" A few snickers follow and I bite my lip, stopping a laugh from bursting out myself.

"It's okay, I got this." Rylee comes to save the day. Stepping up, she lifts her top, exposing her bra, and also fabulous tits. This woman is perfection, but that's besides the fact. Next, she flips her bra strap up from under her arm. "Do you see it?" she asks.

I lean closer to her and see faintly, a small scar decorating the side of her ribs, just under her armpit. The shape reminds me of a snake with maybe a circle or letter *D* underneath, it's hard to tell.

"Our original founding members did this days after founding our organization, the society. And now it's your turn. It's sacred, share this only with someone you can trust into death. As we are now trusting you with our lives."

Sitting back, the responsibility of hundreds of people's lives now weighs heavily on my shoulders. Doubt tries to cross my mind, but I don't allow it to linger. I've trained for this moment my entire fucking life. I can do this.

The crunching of grass catching my attention. Looking toward the noise, Lucy is making her way over to me. In head to toe black like the others, her hair is long, cascading over her shoulders, and a giant smile adorns her face. She seems far too excited for my liking, just as sadistic as I am, in her own way. Standing in front of me now, she boxes me in, placing her hands on the armrests. "Left or right?" she asks.

I look back at her, confused, and hesitantly respond with, "Left?"

Lifting one hand, her finger brushes against my bare skin, pushing my hair over my shoulder. Goosebumps follow and I am so fucking embarrassed that my body is betraying me.

Once satisfied, she reaches behind her and pulls out a

blade. It shines beautifully under the moonlight and my body is now giddy with excitement. I love where this could be going, naughty bitch.

Lifting her hand, she places the sharp tip into my exposed skin and presses in deep, then she starts cutting. The sting, the parting of flesh, and the feeling of my warm blood beginning to drip down my body, feels so fucking good, it's euphoric.

Her body leans farther into mine, and her mouth moves, whispering sweet words. "This is how the adults play."

I smile at her statement and continue to feel the release she is giving me. I don't look down, I don't watch her work. I focus on her face. Lucy's eyes squint slightly, she loves this just as much as I do, as her lips part and her head tilts.

She is a woman dedicated to the craft.

"Your family didn't want to make you bleed. They asked me to do the honors and I gladly accepted. To make you bleed, at my mercy. How could I say no?" She speaks with such mischief, and the wink at the end only adds to her allure.

Lucy's focus returns to my chest. I think the snake is done as I feel her adjust the blade and start the next portion. Taking the opportunity of her being occupied, I rasp the words to a classic song, "Say my name, it tastes good rolling off your tongue."

This causes her to pause. We stay like this for a

moment longer, at a standstill of sorts, until she responds. "No."

Interesting.

Taking a deep breath, I catch her scent, and it is delicious, cupcakes. The woman smells of delicious fucking cupcakes. My mouth waters as I picture stacks of cupcakes. Captivated, I watch as she steps back then slices her hand with the same knife she just used on me. Squeezing her palm tight, Lucy holds it over my brand, letting droplets of her blood mix with mine. The act is sensual. Others join us and she passes the knife around. One by one they do the same notion, allowing our blood to mix, like Blaise and I did all those years ago.

Mom steps up just before Dad, who is last, and mouths, "I am so proud of you." And I could explode into a ball of emotions at any second now.

Dad passes the pigs' leashes back to Mom and he greets me last. I notice he also didn't take the blade from Mom, instead pulling out his own, of course. He's so particular. Cutting his hand, he follows suit, squeezing his into mine, and says, "Baby Sin." A nickname he gave me as a baby, which stayed with me my entire life. And the tears are back. Dammit.

Mom joins him now, standing side by side. Reaching forward, she passes me my babies' leashes and they come to sit on either side of me on my throne. I briefly look down at my chest, the slithering *S* has a letter *D* prominently underneath.

Papa speaks up. "For most, it means Devil's Society,

for you and I, it means Diablo. Wear it with pride, Sid. It's yours now." A bright flash follows, nearly blinding me, before I realize it's someone taking a photo. Then it occurs to me that Greta was on her best behavior tonight and I am shocked and kind of disappointed. We can always count on her for making serious moments lighter.

Staying seated for a few moments longer, I watch as buckets of water douse the flames. Comforting sizzles relax me.

Papa stays by my side, and I look up at him to ask, "Are you sad?"

His head shakes. "No. I'm not sure what I am yet. But it's not sadness."

Good, I'm glad, because it would break my heart knowing this was harder on him than anticipated. Placing his hand on my shoulder, I say "Shall we?"

"I suppose so."

"Thank you for tonight. For my childhood, for all our special moments. You helped shape me into the person I am today, and for that, I am forever grateful to you, Papa." I barely get the words out without a lump of emotion erupting from within.

Squeezing my shoulder, his voice is hushed, his words are little, but they stretch miles in meaning. "Always, Sid. Always."

"She was Dalton's daughter. Abi," I finally muster up the courage to tell him. Plus, it's too late for him to change his mind about Diablo.

But he doesn't get mad, his demeanor remains unchanged. "I'm proud of you."

Then we are interrupted. "Let's go old man," Rylee teases, making me smile.

Papa whispers, "That's my cue," and takes off toward his queen.

Rising, I walk with the group, my pigs following alongside me as I bask in this space, this moment in time one last time, before shouting behind me, "Greta, you're coming with me. Sorry, guys. She's all mine for the rest of the night." Jack and Sally snort in agreement. I need her smart-ass mouth to help balance this heavy, therapeutic emotional night. I can hear her walker click behind me and I smile as she follows.

We get into the Bentley, and after loading up the babies and Greta's walker, I look up to the sky. You can start to see bright oranges and pinks appearing from behind the snow capped mountains. Forest climbs halfway up them and surrounds this beautiful open space. Then, in absolute disbelief, it occurs to me that it must be morning.

Turning the car on, the clock reveals it's five thirty. Fuck me.

"I'm fucking tired. Get moving. I don't care if you are the fucking Diablo or that hot pirate from those Caribbean movies. Get moving so I can go to bed."

I burst out laughing at her completely random comparison. "You got it, G."

Once she's done coughing up a lung, she retorts, "Don't fucking call me that. Now drive, girl."

Reversing out, an unknown number calls my phone. I am hesitant to answer, but do so anyway on my Bluetooth. "Yes?"

"The church! Fuck, Sid." I don't recognize the voice on the other end but it's frantic, and as I am about to question them, loud sirens echo through my speakers. With a racing heart, realization overwhelms me.

Shit.

Straight away, I try to gather the million moving parts and one psychopath so I can strategically analyze my next moves, and fast. Dust clouds around us, and as it clears, I can see my dad's Range Rover peeling out of here.

He knows.

Who fucking called him? I bet it was that priest. Guy is terrified of my dad.

Hanging up immediately on the unknown caller, I dial Uncle Thomas while Greta sits quietly listening.

"Sid. The church. It's bad."

I don't let him finish. "Find him! Find my brother. Please. Keep him safe and bring him to me. Alive. Before my dad can get to him."

Uncle Thomas sighs. "Understood."

I understand the position this puts him in, but it's what's right. It's what I have instructed. Pulling rank the first ten minutes of being Diablo wasn't something I was planning, but I have to. He's my brother, and I must keep him safe. Worry runs my brain rampant.

Squeezing my eyes shut, I silently speak to myself. *Please, Uncle Thomas, to get to him. Please, before my dad does.*

Greta speaks up. My eyes open at her ominous tone, bringing reality back to the forefront. "Honey, your daddy is ten steps ahead. Your brother is as good as dead."

BLAISE

"I'm not hiding, Dad. Come and get me, I'm right fucking here."

My arms are wide open, with bright, hot flames as my backdrop. The church is hundreds of years old, and the moment I lit the first old wooden pew inside, it spread rapidly and flames engulfed the place in minutes. Looking up momentarily, black smoke blocks the view of the morning sun. What a shame.

Then tires squeal against the pavement. The smell of burning rubber joins the overwhelming smell of smoke from the church.

I look over, it's a black Range. Grinning, my body vibrates with adrenaline.

It's time to play. The battle to end all battles.

I am about to play the deadliest game of chicken with a psychopath.

My dad.

BLAISE
EPILOGUE

"How long do I have to stay here?" I ask my sister, the new queen bee of the society.

Placing her scarred palm against the bulletproof glass, I notice the significance but can't find it in me to give a fuck. Sid is trying to pull at my emotions, emotions which I do not contain for anyone else but *her* and possibly Mom, and that is a big fucking maybe.

The phone is pressed tightly against Sid's ear. "Until it's safe for you to come out."

Her voice speaks as if she is feeling pain and sadness regarding the situation, but like everyone else, I'm sure they are happy to be rid of me.

"And you think he can't get me in here?" I laugh hysterically through the other end. What a fucking joke, my dad and the society can get anywhere they want.

She is quick to jump in and reassure me. "He won't. It would hurt Mom; it would hurt me. Dad won't risk that...

plus, he would have to find you first..." And at this point I think Sid is trying to convince herself of that too. She needs to wake the fuck up and realize I am not dead because he doesn't want me dead, yet, but it's coming. Unless...

My laughter continues, echoing off the white cylinder block walls, as I realize what she's done. Well fucking done, sis.

"He doesn't know? You are so screwed when he finds out you have been hiding me," I taunt.

If my dad wants me dead, he won't sleep until it happens.

"Sid, fuck you. Fuck the institution you are so desperate to fit into, fuck the family."

I drop the phone on the wooden desk before me and stand, showing off my orange jumpsuit along with my prisoner number, 00881306. The newest inmate at Bozeman Correctional Center.

"Guard, I'm done here," I shout, banging on the glass so I can be escorted back to my cozy cell for two. The guy may as well take me to the green mile, because my days are fucking numbered.

He can get to me from anywhere.

THE END.

WHAT'S NEXT?

Reckless
The Grand Finale of
The Devil's Society
A Dark MM Romance
Coming Soon!

ALSO BY KINSLEY KINCAID

FORBIDDEN

Let's Play

Within the Shadows

Lessons from the Depraved

Haunted by the Devil; The Devil's Society

Sinner; The Devil's Society

Homecoming; The Devil's Society

Unholy; The Devil's Society

Sweet SIN Slaughterhouse; The Devil's Society

Reckless; The Devil's Society - Coming Soon!

TABOO

Wrecked

Sutton Asylum

Sick Obsession

Dark Temptation: Part One

Ghost Dick; A Port Canyon Chronicle

Dark Temptation: Part Two

Lessons; An Extremely Fucking Taboo Extended Epilogue

Brothers Bond

Fuck Me, Daddy; A Port Canyon Chronicle - TBD

ABOUT THE AUTHOR

Kinsley is a Canadian, Dark Romance Author who dabbles in Taboo, Forbidden, Paranormal and is currently in her Erotic Horror Era. When she isn't plotting her next twisted book or watching true crime docs with her cats, you can find her working for the man. Reading. Or listening to Taylor Swift & Sleep Token.

Make sure you follow Kins on her socials and sign up for her newsletter to see what is coming next!

authorkinsleykincaid.com